FICTION HOUSE PRESS PRESENTS

INFINITY SCIENCE FICTION

March 1958
Vol. 3, No. 3

This reprint edition is a facsimile of the original pulp magazine. Variations in printing and quality can be attributed to the original magazine which was printed on rough woodpulp paper. No attempt has been made to politically correct any language deemed inappropriate to the modern reader.

ISBN 978-1-64720-379-5

www.FictionHousePress.com
fictionhousepress@gmail.com

That's Right—
I Said *Three* Copies!

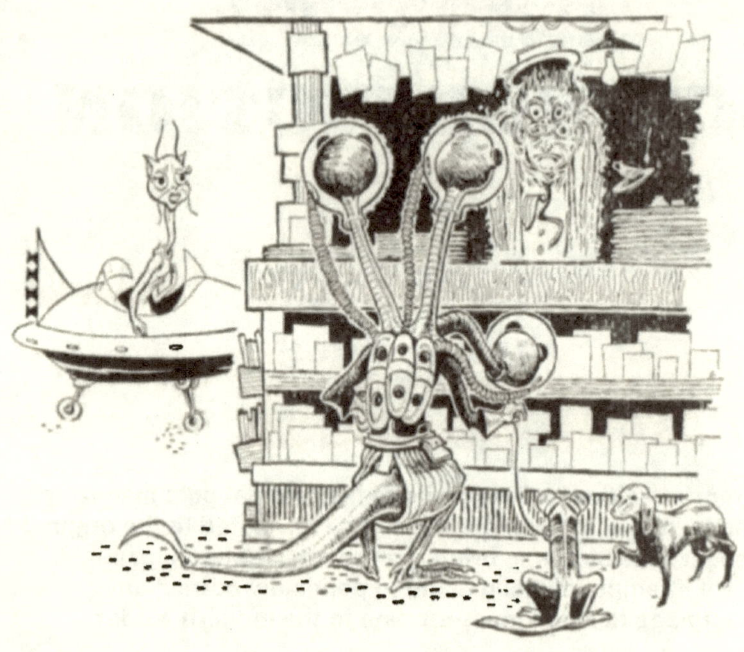

Of course we love customers like this, who buy three copies of every issue of *Infinity* and *Science Fiction Adventures*—one for each head!

But then, we love all our customers, even those who only buy one copy of every issue. In fact, we'd be perfectly happy if everybody in the universe just bought one copy of every issue.

As it is, we're happy to please the customers we've got—because they're the people (and monsters) who know that *Infinity* and *SFA* consistently publish the best science fiction available. In short, they're the most intelligent people (and monsters) in the universe!

Remember, monsters of distinction have subscriptions. See full details inside.

SCIENCE FICTION

March, 1958

Vol. 3, No. 3

THE MAGAZINE OF TOMORROWNESS

Novelet:

Stories:

Two-Part Novel:

Departments:

COVER, illustrating *Accept No Substitutes*, by Ed Emsh

ILLUSTRATIONS by Bill Bowman, Ed Emsh and Richard Kluga.

INFINITY SCIENCE FICTION, published monthly except for February, August, and December, by Royal Publications, Inc., 11 West 42nd Street, New York 36, N. Y. Single copy 35¢; subscription (12 issues) for the U. S., its territories and possessions, and Canada, $3.50; elsewhere, $4.50. Second-class mail privileges authorized at New York, N. Y.

Printed in U. S. A.

Illustrated by BILL BOWMAN

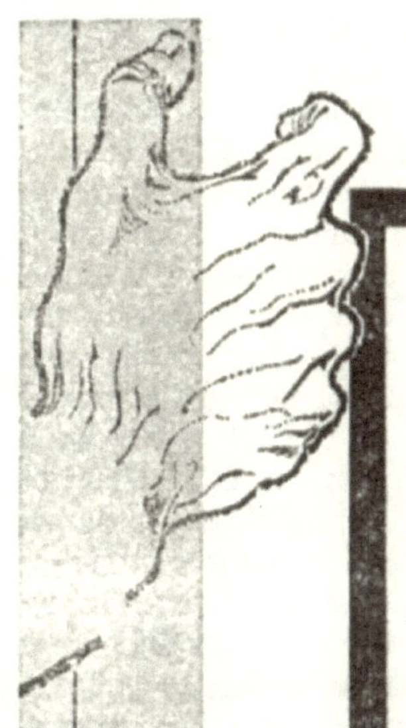

THE SUN had gone down blood-red, and Colonel John Devall slept poorly because of it. The atmosphere on Markin was not normally conducive to blood-red sunsets, though they did happen occasionally on evenings when the blue of sunlight was scattered particularly well. The Marks connected red sunsets with approaching trouble. Colonel Devall, who headed the Terran cultural and military mission to Markin, was more cultural than military himself, and so was willing to accept the Markin belief that the sunset was a premonition of conflict.

The Overlord's Thumb

By ROBERT SILVERBERG

His choice would govern a boy's fate— and, incidentally, Earth's entire future

He was tall, well-made and erect in bearing, with the sharp bright eyes and crisp manner of the military man. He successfully tried to project an appearance of authoritative officerhood, and his men respected and feared the image he showed them.

His degree was in anthropology. The military education was an afterthought, but a shrewd one; it had brought him command of the Markin outpost. The Department of Extraterrestrial Affairs insisted that all missions to relatively primitive alien worlds be staffed and headed by military men—and, Devall reasoned, so long as I keep up the outward show, who's to know that I'm not the tough soldier they think I am? Markin was a peaceful enough world. The natives were intelligent, fairly highly advanced culturally if not technically, easily dealt with on a rational being-to-being basis.

Which explains why Devall slept badly the night of the red sun. Despite his elegant posture and comportment, he regarded himself essentially as a bookish, un-military man. He had some doubts as to his own possible behavior in an unforeseen time of crisis. The false front of his officerhood might well crumble away under stress, and he knew it.

He dozed off, finally, toward morning, having kicked the covers to the floor and twisted the sheets into crumpled confusion. It was a warmish night—most of them were, on Markin—but he felt chilled.

He woke late, only a few minutes before officers' mess, and dressed hurriedly in order to get there on time. As commanding officer, of course, he had the privilege of sleeping as late as he pleased—but getting up with the others was part of the task Devall imposed on himself. He donned the light summer uniform, slapped depilator hastily on his tanned face, hooked on his formal blaster and belt, and signalled to his orderly that he was awake and ready.

The Terran enclave covered ten acres, half an hour's drive from one of the largest Markin villages. An idling jeep waited outside Devall's small private dome, and he climbed in, nodding curtly at the orderly.

"Morning, Harris."

"Good morning, sir. Sleep well?"

It was a ritual by now. "Very well," Devall responded automatically, as the jeep's turbos thrummed once and sent the little car humming across the compound to the mess hall. Clipped to the seat next to Devall was his daily morning program-sheet, prepared for him by the staffman-of-the-day while he slept. This morning's sheet was signed by Dudley, a major of formidable efficiency—Space Service through and through, a Military Wing career man and nothing else. Devall scanned the assignments for the morning, neatly written out in Dudley's crabbed hand.

Kelly, Dorfman, Mellors, Steber on Linguistic Detail, as usual. Same assignment as yesterday, in town.

Haskell on medic duty. Blood samples; urinalysis.

Matsuoko to maintenance staff (through Wednesday).

Jolli on zoo detail.

Leonards, Meyer, Rodriguez on assigned botanical field trip, two days. Extra jeep assigned for specimen collection.

Devall scanned the rest of the list, but, as expected, Dudley had done a perfect job of deploying the men where they would be most useful and most happy. Devall thought briefly about Leonards, on the botanical field trip. A two-day trip might take them through the dangerous rain-forest to the south; Devall felt a faint flicker of worry. The boy was his nephew, his sister's son—a reasonably competent journeyman botanist with the gold bar still untarnished on his shoulder. This was the boy's first commission; he had been assigned to Devall's unit at random, as a new man. Devall had concealed his relationship to Leonards from the other men, knowing it might make things awkward for the boy, but he still felt a protective urge.

Hell, the kid can take care of himself, Devall thought, and scribbled his initials at the bottom of the sheet and clipped it back in place; it would be posted while the men were cleaning their quarters and the officers ate, and by 0900 everyone would be out on his day's assignment. There was so much to do, Devall thought, and so little time to do it. There were so many worlds—

He quitted the jeep and entered the mess h.ll. Officers' mess was a small well-lit alcove to the left of the main hall; as Devall entered he saw seven men standing stiffly at attention, waiting for him.

He knew they hadn't been standing that way all morning; they had snapped to attention only when their lookout—probably Second Lieutenant Leonards, the youngest—had warned them he was coming.

Well, he thought, it doesn't matter much. As long as appearance is preserved. The form.

"Good morning, gentlemen," he said crisply, and took his place at the head of the table.

For a while, it looked as if it were going to turn out a pretty good day. The sun rose in a cloudless sky, and the thermometer tacked to the enclave flagstaff registered 93 degrees. When Markin got hot, it got *hot.* By noon, Devall knew by now, they could expect something like 110 in the shade—and then, a slow, steady decline into the low eighties by midnight.

The botanical crew departed on time, rumbling out of camp in its two jeeps, and Devall stood for a moment on the mess hall steps watching them go, watching the other men head for their assigned posts. Stubble-faced Sergeant Jolli saluted him as he trotted across the compound to the zoo, where he would tend the little menagerie of Markin wildlife the expedition would bring back to Earth at termination. Wiry little Matsuoko passed by, dragging a carpenter's kit. The linguistic team climbed into its jeep and drove off toward town, where they would continue their studies in the Markin tongue.

They were all busy. The expedition had been on Markin just four months; eight months was left of their time. Unless an extension of stay came through, they'd pack up and return to Earth for six months of furlough-cum-report-session, and then it would be on to some other world for another year of residence.

Devall was not looking forward to leaving Markin. It was a pleasant world, if a little on the hot side, and there was no way of knowing what the *next* world would be like. A frigid ball of frozen methane, perhaps, where they would spend their year bundled into Valdez breathing-suits and trying to make contact with some species of intelligent ammonia-breathing molluscs. Better the devil we know, Devall felt.

But he had to keep moving on. This was his eleventh world, and there would be more to come. Earth had barely enough qualified survey teams to cover ten thousand worlds half-adequately, and life abounded on ten *million.* He would retain whichever members of the current team satisfied him by their performance, replace those who didn't fit in, and go off to his next job eight months from now.

He turned on the office fan and took down the logbook; unfastening the binder, he slipped the first blank sheet into the autotype. For once he avoided his standard blunder; he cleared his throat *before* switching on the autotype, thereby sparing the machine its customary difficulties in finding a verbal equivalent for his *Brghhumph!*

The guidelight glowed a soft red. Devall said, "Fourth April, two-seven-zero-five. Colonel John F. Devall recording. One hundred nineteenth day of our stay on Markin, World 7 of System 1106-sub-a.

"Temperature, 93 at 0900; wind gentle, southerly—"

He went on at considerable length, as he did each morning. Finishing off the required details, he gathered up the sheaf of specialty-reports that had been left at his door the night before, and began to read abstracts into the log; the autotype clattered merrily, and a machine somewhere in the basement of the towering E-T Affairs Building in Rio de Janeiro was reproducing his words as the sub-radio hookup transmitted them.

It was dull work. Devall often wondered whether he might have been ultimately happier doing simple anthropological field work, as he had once done, instead of taking on the onerous burden of routine that an administrative post entailed. *But someone has to shoulder the burden,* he thought.

Earthman's burden. We're the most advanced race; we help the others. But no one twists our arms to come out to these worlds and share what we have. Call it an inner compulsion.

He intended to work until noon; in the afternoon a Markin high priest was coming to the enclave to see him, and the interview would probably take almost till sundown. But about 1100 he was interrupted suddenly by the sound of jeeps unexpectedly entering the compound, and he heard the clamor of voices—both Terran voices and alien ones.

A fearful argument seemed to be in progress, but the group was too far away and Devall's knowledge of Markin too uncertain for him to be able to tell what was causing the rumpus. In some annoyance he snapped off the autotype, rose from his chair, and peered through the window into the yard.

Two jeeps had drawn up—the botanical crew, gone less than two hours. Four natives surrounded the three Earthmen. Two of the natives clutched barbed spears; a third was a woman, the fourth an old man. They were all protesting hotly over something.

Devall scowled; from the pale, tense, unhappy faces of the men in the jeep, he could tell something was very wrong. That blood-red sunset had foretold accurately, he thought, as he dashed down the steps from his study.

Seven pairs of eyes focussed on him as he strode toward the group: eight glittering alien eyes, warmly golden, and six shifting, uneasy Terran eyes.

"What's going on out here?" Devall demanded.

The aliens set up an immediate babble of noise, chattering away like a quartet of squirrels. Devall had never seen any of them behaving this way before.

"Quiet!" he roared.

In the silence that followed he said very softly, "Lieutenant Leonards, can you tell me exactly what all this fuss is about?"

The boy looked very frightened; his jaws were stiffly clenched, his lips bloodless. "Y-yes, sir," he said stammeringly. "Begging your pardon, sir. I seem to have killed an alien."

In the relative privacy of his office, Devall faced them all again—Leonards, sitting very quietly staring at his gleaming boots; Meyer and Rodriguez, who had accompanied him on the ill-starred botanizing journey. The aliens were outside; there would be time to calm them down later.

"Okay," Devall said. "Leonards, I want you to repeat the story, exactly as you just told it to me, and I'll get it down on the autotype. Start talking when I point to you."

He switched on the autotype and said, "Testimony of Second Lieutenant Paul Leonards, Botanist, delivered in presence of commanding officer on 4 April 2705." He jabbed a forefinger at Leonards.

The boy's face looked waxy, beads of sweat dotted his pale vein-traced forehead, and his blond hair was tangled and twisted. He clamped his lips together in an agonized grimace, scratched the back of one hand, and finally said, "Well, we left the enclave about 0900 this morning, bound south and westerly on a tour of the outlying regions. Our purpose was to collect botanical specimens. I—was in charge of the group, which also included Sergeants Meyer and Rodriguez."

He paused. "We—we accomplished little in the first half-hour; this immediate area had already been thoroughly covered by us anyway. But about 0945 Meyer noticed a heavily wooded area not far to the left of the main road, and called it to my attention. I suggested we stop and investigate. It was impossible to penetrate the wooded area in our jeeps, so we proceeded on foot. I left Rodriguez to keep watch over our gear while we were gone.

"We made our way through a close-packed stand of deciduous angiosperm trees of a species we had already studied, and found ourselves in a secluded area of natural growth, including several species which we could see were previously uncatalogued. We found one in particular—a shrub consisting of a single thick succulent green stalk perhaps four feet high, topped by a huge gold and green composite flower head. We filmed it in detail, took scent samples, pollen prints, and removed several leaves."

Devall broke in suddenly. "You didn't pick the flower itself? Devall speaking."

"Of course not. It was the only specimen in the vicinity, and it's not our practice to destroy single specimens for the sake of collecting. But I did remove several leaves from the stalk. And the moment I did that, a native sprang at me from behind a thick clump of ferns.

"He was armed with one of those notched spears. Meyer saw him first and yelled, and I jumped back just as the alien came charging forward with his spear. I managed to deflect the spear with the outside of my arm and was not hurt. The alien fell back a few feet and shouted something at me in his language, which I don't understand too well as yet. Then he raised his spear and menaced me with it. I was carrying the standard-issue radial blaster. I drew it and ordered him in his own language to lower his spear, that we meant no harm. He ignored me and charged a second time. I fired in self-defense, trying to destroy the spear or at worst wound his arm, but he spun round to take the full force of the charge, and died instantly." Leonards shrugged. "That's about it, sir. We came back here instantly."

"Umm. Devall speaking. Sergeant Meyer, would you say this account is substantially true?"

Meyer was a thin-faced dark-haired man who was usually smiling, but he wasn't smiling now. "This is Sergeant Meyer. I'd say that Lieutenant Leonards told the story substantially as it occurred. Except that the alien didn't seem overly fierce despite his actions, in my opinion. I myself thought he was bluffing both times he charged, and I was a little surprised when Lieutenant Leonards shot him. That's all, sir."

Frowning, the colonel said, "Devall speaking. This has been testimony in the matter of the alien killed today by Lieutenant Leonards." He snapped off the autotype, stood up, and leaned forward across the desk, staring sternly at the trio of young botanists facing him. *These next few days are going to be my test,* he thought tensely.

"Sergeant Rodriguez, since you weren't present at the actual incident I'll consider you relieved of all responsibility in this matter, and your testimony won't be required. Report to Major Dudley for re-assignment for the remainder of the week."

"Thank you, sir." Rodriguez saluted, grinned gratefully, and was gone.

"As for you two, though," Devall said heavily, "you'll both have to be confined to base pending the outcome of the affair. I don't need to tell you how serious this can be, whether the killing was in self-defense or not. Plenty of peoples don't understand the concept of self-defense." He moistened his suddenly dry lips. "I don't anticipate too many complications growing out of this. But these are alien people on an alien world, and their behavior is never certain."

He glanced at Leonards. "Lieutenant, I'll have to ask for your own safety that you remain in your quarters until further notice."

"Yes, sir. Is this to be considered arrest?"

"Not yet," Devall said. "Meyer, attach yourself to the

maintenance platoon for the remainder of the day. We'll probably need your testimony again before this business is finished. Dismissed, both of you."

When they were gone, Devall sank back limply in his webfoam chair and stared at his fingertips. His hands were quivering as if they had a life of their own.

John F. Devall, Ph.D. Anthropology Columbia '82, commissioned Space Service Military Wing '87, and now you're in trouble for the first time.

How are you going to handle it, Jack? he asked himself. *Can you prove that that silver eagle really belongs on your shoulder?*

He was sweating. He felt very tired. He shut his eyes for a moment, opened them, and said into the intercom, "Send in the Marks."

FIVE OF THEM entered, made ceremonial bows, and ranged themselves nervously along the far wall as if they were firing-squad candidates. Accompanying them came Steber of the linguistics team, hastily recalled from town to serve as an interpreter for Devall. The colonel's knowledge of Markin was adequate but sketchy; he wanted Steber around in case any fine points had to be dealt with in detail.

The Marks were humanoid in structure, simian in ancestry, which should have made them close kin to the Terrans in general physiological structure. They weren't. Their skin was a rough, coarse, pebble-grained affair, dark-toned, running to muddy browns and occasional deep purples. Their jaws had somehow acquired a reptilian hinge in the course of evolution, which left them practically chinless but capable of swallowing food in huge lumps that would strangle an Earthman. Their eyes, liquid gold in color, were set wide on their heads, allowing enormous peripheral vision; their noses were flat buttons, in some cases barely perceptible.

Devall saw two younger men, obviously warriors; they had left their weapons outside, but their jaws jutted belligerently and the darker of the pair had virtually dislocated his jaw in rage. The woman looked like all the Mark women, shapeless and weary behind her shabby cloak of furs. The remaining pair were priests, one old, one *very* old. It was this ancient to whom Devall addressed his first remarks.

"I'm sorry that our meeting this afternoon has to be one of sorrow. I had been looking forward to a pleasant talk. But it's not always possible to predict what lies ahead."

"Death lay ahead for him who was killed," the old priest said in the dry, high-pitched tone of voice that Devall knew implied anger and scorn.

The woman let out a sudden wild ululation, half a dozen wailing words jammed together so rapidly Devall could not translate them. "What did she say?" he asked Steber.

The interpreter flattened his palms together thoughtfully. "She's the woman of the man who was killed. She was—demanding revenge," he said in English.

Apparently the two young warriors were friends of the dead man. Devall's eyes scanned the five hostile alien faces. "This is a highly regrettable incident," he said in Markin. "But I trust it won't affect the warm relationship between Earthman and Markin that has prevailed so far. This misunderstanding—"

"Blood must be atoned," said the smaller and less impressively garbed of the two priests. He was probably the local priest, Devall thought, and he was probably happy to have his superior on hand to back him up.

The colonel flicked sweat from his forehead. "The young man who committed the act will certainly be disciplined. Of course you realize that a killing in self-defense cannot be regarded as murder, but I admit the young man did act unwisely and will suffer the consequences." It didn't sound too satisfying to Devall, and, indeed, the aliens hardly seemed impressed.

The high priest uttered two short, sharp syllables. They were not words in Devall's vocabulary, and he looked over at Steber in appeal.

"He said Leonards was trespassing on sacred ground. He said the crime they're angry about is not murder but blasphemy."

Despite the heat, Devall felt a sudden chill. *Not . . . murder? This is going to be complicated,* he realized gloomily.

To the priest he said, "Does this change the essential nature of the case? He'll still be punished by us for his action, which can't be condoned."

"You may punish him for murder, if you so choose," the high priest said, speaking very slowly, so Devall would understand each word. The widow emitted some highly terrestrial-sounding sobs; the young men glowered stolidly. "Murder is not our concern," the high priest went on. "He has taken life; life belongs to Them, and They withdraw it whenever They see fit, by whatever means They care to employ. But he has also desecrated a sacred flower on sacred ground. These are serious crimes, to us. Added to this he has shed the blood of a Guardian, on sacred ground. We ask you to turn him over to us for trial by a priestly court on this double charge of blasphemy. Afterward, perhaps, you may try him by your own laws, for whichever one of them he has broken."

For an instant all Devall saw was the old priest's implacable leathery face; then he turned and caught the expression of white-faced astonishment and dismay Steber displayed.

It took several seconds for the high priest's words to sink in, and several more before Devall came to stunned realization of the implications. *They want to try an Earthman,* he thought numbly. *By their own law. In their own court. And mete out their own punishment.*

This had abruptly ceased being a mere local incident, an affair to clean up, note in the log, and forget. It was no longer a matter of simple reparations for the accidental killing of an alien.

Now, thought Devall dully, it was a matter of galactic importance. And he was the man who had to make all the decisions.

HE VISITED Leonards that evening, after the meal. By that time everyone in the camp knew what had happened, though Devall had ordered Steber to keep quiet about the alien demand to try Leonards themselves.

The boy looked up as Devall entered his room, and managed a soggy salute.

"At ease, Lieutenant." Devall sat on the edge of Leonards' bed and squinted up at him. "Son, you're in very hot water now."

"Sir, I—"

"I know. You didn't mean to pluck leaves off the sacred bramble-bush, and you couldn't help shooting down the native who attacked you. And if this business were as simple as all that, I'd reprimand you for hotheadedness and let it go at that. But—"

"But what, sir?"

Devall scowled and forced himself to face the boy squarely. "But the aliens want to try you themselves. They aren't so much concerned with the murder as they are with your double act of blasphemy. That withered old high priest wants to take you before an ecclesiastical court."

"You won't allow *that,* of course, will you, Colonel?" Leonards seemed confident that such an unthinkable thing could never happen.

"I'm not so sure, Paul," Devall said quietly, deliberately using the boy's first name.

"*What,* sir?"

"This is evidently something very serious you've committed. That high priest is calling a priestly convocation to deal with you. They'll be back here to get you tomorrow at noon, he said."

"But you wouldn't turn me over to them, sir! After all, I was on duty; I had no knowledge of the offense I was committing. Why, it's none of their business!"

"Make *them* see that," Devall said flatly. "They're aliens. They don't understand Terran legal codes. They don't *want* to hear about our laws; by theirs, you've blasphemed, and blasphemers must be punished. This is a law-abiding race on Markin. They're an ethically advanced society, regardless of the fact that they're not technologically advanced. Ethically they're on the same plane we are."

Leonards looked terribly pale. "You'll turn me over to them?"

Devall shrugged. "I didn't say that. But look at it from my position. I'm leader of a cultural and military mission. Our purpose is to live among these people, learn their ways, guide them as much as we can in our limited time here. We at least *try* to make a pretense of respecting their rights as individuals and as a species, you know.

"Well, now it's squarely on the line. Are we friends living among them and helping them, or are we overlords grinding them under our thumbs?"

"Sir, I'd say that was an oversimplification," Leonards remarked hesitantly.

"Maybe so. But the issue's clear enough. If we turn them down, it means we're setting up a gulf of superiority between Earth and these aliens, despite the big show we made about being brothers. And word will spread to other planets. We try to sound like friends, but our actions in the celebrated Leonards case reveal our true colors. We're arrogant, imperialistic, patronizing, and—well, do you see?"

"So you're going to turn me over to them for trial, then," the boy said quietly.

Devall shook his head. He felt old, very old, at fifty. "I don't know. I haven't made up my mind yet. If I turn you over, it'll certainly set a dangerous precedent. And if I don't—I'm not sure what will happen." He shrugged. "I'm going to refer the case back to Earth. It isn't my decision to make."

BUT it *was* his decision to make, he thought, as he left the boy's quarters and headed stiff-legged toward the communications shack. He was on the spot, and only he could judge the complex of factors that controlled the case. Earth would almost certainly pass the buck back to him.

He was grateful for one thing, though: at least Leonards hadn't made an appeal to him on family grounds. That was cause for pride, and some relief. The fact that the boy was his nephew was something he'd have to blot rigorously from his mind until all this was over.

The signalman was busy in the back of the shack, bent over a crowded worktable. Devall waited a moment, cleared his throat gently, and said, "Mr. Rory?"

Rory turned. "Yes, Colonel?"

"Put through a subradio solido to Earth for me, immediately. To Director Thornton at the E-T Department. And yell for me when you've made contact."

It took twenty minutes for the subspace impulse to leap out across the light-years and find a receiver on Earth, ten minutes more for it to pass through the relay point and on to Rio. Devall returned to the shack to find the lambent green solido field in tune and waiting for him. He stepped through and discovered himself standing a few feet before the desk of the E-T Department's head. Thornton's image was sharp, but the desk seemed to waver at the edges. Solid non-organic objects always came through poorly.

Quickly Devall reviewed the situation. Thornton sat patiently, unmoving, till the end of it; hands knotted rigidly, lean face set, he might have been a statue. Finally he commented, "Unpleasant business."

"Quite."

"The alien is returning tomorrow, you say? I'm afraid that doesn't give us much time to hold a staff meeting and explore the problem, Colonel Devall."

"I could probably delay him a few days."

Thornton's thin lips formed a tight bloodless line. After an instant he said, "No. Take whatever action you deem necessary, Colonel. If the psychological pattern of the race is such that unfortunate consequences would result if you refused to allow them to try your man, then you must certainly turn him over. If the step can be avoided, of course, avoid it. The man must be punished in any case."

The director smiled bleakly. "You're one of our best men, Colonel. I'm confident you'll arrive at an ultimately satisfactory resolution to this incident."

"Thank you, sir," Devall said, in a dry, uncertain voice. He nodded and stepped back out of field range. Thornton's image seemed to flicker; Devall caught one last dismissing sentence, "Report back to me when the matter is settled," and then the field died.

He stood alone in the shabby communications shack, blinking out the sudden darkness that rolled in over him after the solidophone's intense light, and after a moment began to pick his way over the heaps of equipment and out into the compound.

It was as he had expected. Thornton was a good man, but he was a civilian appointee, subject to government control. He disliked making top-level decisions—particularly when a colonel a few hundred light-years away could be pitchforked into making them for him.

Well, he thought, *at least I notified Earth. The rest of the affair is in my hands.*

Significantly, there was a red sunset again that night.

HE CALLED a meeting of his top staff men for 0915 the following morning. Work at the base had all but suspended; the linguistics team was confined to the area, and Devall had ordered guards posted at all exits. Violence could rise unexpectedly among even the most placid of alien peoples; it was impossible to predict the moment when a racial circuit-breaker would cease to function and fierce hatred burst forth.

They listened in silence to the tapes of Leonards' statements, Meyer's comments, and the brief interview Devall had had with the five aliens. Devall punched the cut-off stud and glanced rapidly round the table at his men: two majors, a captain, and a quartet of lieutenants comprised his high staff, and one of the lieutenants was confined to quarters.

"That's the picture. The old high priest is showing up here about noon for my answer. I thought I'd toss the thing open for staff discussion first."

Major Dudley asked for the floor.

He was a short, stocky man with dark flashing eyes, and on several occasions in the past had been known to disagree violently with Devall on matters of procedure. Devall had picked him for four successive trips, despite this; the colonel believed in diversity of opinion, and Dudley was a tremendously efficient organizer as well.

"Major?"

"Sir, it doesn't seem to me that there's any question of what action to take. It's impossible to hand Leonards over to them for trial. It's—un-Earthlike!"

Devall frowned. "Would you elaborate, Major?"

"Simple enough. We're the race who developed the space-drive—therefore, we're the galaxy's most advanced race. I think that goes without saying."

"It does not," Devall commented. "But go ahead."

Scowling, Dudley said, "Regardless of your opinion, *sir*—the aliens we've encountered so far have all regarded us as their obvious superiors. I don't think that can be denied—and I think it can only be attributed to the fact that we *are* their superiors. Well, if we give up Leonards for trial, it cheapens our position. It makes us look weak, spineless. We—"

"You're suggesting, then," Devall broke in, "that we hold the position of overlords in the galaxy—and by yielding to our serfs, we may lose all control over them. Is this your belief, Major?" Devall glared at him.

Dudley met the colonel's angry gaze calmly. "Basically, yes. Dammit, sir, I've tried to make you see this ever since the Hegath expedition. We're not out here in the stars to collect butterflies and squirrels! We—"

"Out of order," Devall snapped coldly. "This is a cultural mission as well as a military, Major—and so long as I'm in command it remains primarily cultural." He felt on the verge of losing his temper. He glanced away from Dudley and said, "Major Grey, could I hear from you?"

Grey was the ship's astrogator; on land his functions were to supervise stockade-construction and mapmaking. He was a wiry, unsmiling little man with razor-like cheekbones and ruddy skin. "I feel we have to be cautious, sir. Handing Leonards over would result in a tremendous loss of Terran prestige."

"Loss?" Dudley burst in. "It would cripple us! We'd never be able to hold our heads up honestly in the galaxy again if—"

Calmly Devall said, "Major Dudley, you've been ruled out of order. Leave this meeting, Major. I'll discuss a downward revision of your status with you later." Turning back to Grey without a further glance at Dudley, he said, "You don't believe, Major, that such an action would have a corresponding *favorable* effect on our prestige in the eyes of those worlds inclined to regard Earth uneasily?"

"That's an extremely difficult thing to determine, sir."

"Very well, then." Devall rose. "Pursuant to regulations, I've brought this matter to the attention of authorities on Earth, and have also offered it for open discussion among my officers. Thanks for your time, gentlemen."

Captain Marechal said uncertainly, "Sir, won't there be any vote on our intended course of action?"

Devall grinned coldly. "As commanding officer of this base, I'll take the sole responsibility upon myself for the decision in this particular matter. It may make things easier for all of us in the consequent event of a court-martial inquiry."

It was the only way, he thought, as he waited tensely in his office for the high priest to arrive. The officers seemed firmly set against any conciliatory action, in the name of Terra's prestige. It was hardly fair for him to make them take responsibility for a decision that might be repugnant to them.

Too bad about Dudley, Devall mused. But insubordination of that sort was insufferable; Dudley would have to be dropped from the unit on their next trip out. If there is any next trip out for me, he added.

The intercom glowed gently. "Yes?"

"Alien delegation is here, sir," said the orderly.

"Don't send them in until I signal."

He strode to the window and looked out. The compound, at first glance, seemed full of aliens. Actually there were only a dozen, he realized, but they were clad in full panoply, bright red and harsh green robes, carrying spears and ornamental swords. Half a dozen enlisted men were watching them nervously from a distance, their hands ready to fly to blasters instantly if necessary.

He weighed the choices one last time.

If he handed Leonards over, the temporary anger of the aliens would be appeased—but perhaps at a long-range cost to Earth's prestige. Devall had long regarded himself as an essentially weak man with a superb instinct for camouflage—but would his yielding to the aliens imply to the universe that all Earth was weak?

On the other hand, he thought, suppose he refused to release Leonards to the aliens. Then he would be, in essence, bringing down the overlord's thumb, letting the universe know that Earthmen were responsible only to themselves and not to the peoples of of the worlds they visited.

Either way, he realized, the standing of Earth in the galaxy's estimation would suffer. One way, they would look like appeasing weaklings; the other, like tyrants. He remembered a definition he had once read: *melodrama is the conflict of right and wrong, tragedy the conflict of right and right.* Both sides were right here. Whichever way he turned, there would be difficulties.

And there was an additional factor: the boy. What if they executed him? Family considerations seemed absurdly picayune at this moment, but still, to hand his own nephew over for possible execution by an alien people—

He took a deep breath, straightened his shoulders, sharpened the hard gaze of his eyes. A glance at the mirror over the bookcase told him he looked every inch the commanding officer; not a hint of the inner conflict showed through.

He depressed the intercom stud. "Send in the high priest. Let the rest of them wait outside."

THE PRIEST looked impossibly tiny and wrinkled, a gnome of a man whose skin was fantastically gullied and mazed by extreme age. He wore a green turban over his hairless head—a mark of deep mourning, Devall knew.

The little alien bowed low, extending his pipestem arms behind his back at a sharp angle, indicating respect. When he straightened, his head craned back sharply, his small round eyes peering directly into Devall's.

"The jury has been selected; the trial is ready to begin. Where is the boy?"

Devall wished fleetingly he could have had the services of an interpreter for this last interview. But that was impossible; this was something he had to face alone, without help.

"The accused man is in his quarters," Devall said slowly. "First I want to ask some questions, old one."

"Ask."

"If I give you the boy to try, will there be any chance of his receiving the death penalty?"

"It is conceivable."

Devall scowled. "Can't you be a little more definite than that?"

"How can we know the verdict before the trial takes place?"

"Let that pass," Devall said, seeing he would get no concrete reply. "Where would you try him?"

"Not far from here."

"Could I be present at the trial?"

"No."

Devall had learned enough of Markin grammar by now to realize that the form of the negative the priest had employed meant literally, I-say-*no*-and-mean-what-I-say. Moistening his lips, he said, "Suppose I should refuse to turn Lieutenant Leonards over to you for trial? How could I expect you people to react?"

There was a long silence. Finally the old priest said, "Would you do such a thing?"

"I'm speaking hypothetically." (Literally, the form was I-speak-on-a-cloud.)

"It would be very bad. We would be unable to purify the sacred garden for many months. Also—" he added a sentence of unfamiliar words. Devall puzzled unsuccessfully over their meaning for nearly a minute.

"What does that mean?" he asked at length. "Phrase it in different words."

"It is the name of a ritual. *I* would have to stand trial in the Earthman's place—and I would die," the priest said simply. "Then my successor would ask you all to go away."

The office seemed very quiet; the only sounds Devall heard were the harsh breathing of the old priest and the off-key chirruping of the cricketlike insects that infested the grass-plot outside the window.

Appeasement, he wondered? *Or the overlord's thumb?*

Suddenly there seemed no doubt at all in his mind of what he should do, and he wondered how he could have hesitated.

"I hear and respect your wishes, old one," he said, in a ritual formula of renunciation Steber had taught him. "The boy is yours. But can I ask a favor?"

"Ask."

"He didn't know he was offending your laws. He meant well; he's sincerely sorry for what he did. He's in your hands, now—

but I want to ask mercy on his behalf. He had no way of knowing he was offending."

"This will be seen at the trial," the old priest said coldly. "If there is to be mercy, mercy will be shown him. I make no promises."

"Very well," Devall said. He reached for a pad and scrawled an order remanding Lieutenant Paul Leonards to the aliens for trial, and signed it with his full name and title. "Here. Give this to the Earthman who let you in. He'll see to it that the boy is turned over to you."

"You are wise," the priest said. He bowed elaborately and made for the door.

"Just one moment," Devall said desperately, as the alien opened the door. "Another question."

"Ask," the priest said.

"You told me you'd take his place if I refused to let you have him. Well, how about another substitute? Suppose—"

"*You* are not acceptable to us," the priest said as if reading Devall's mind, and left.

Five minutes later the colonel glanced out his window and saw the solemn procession of aliens passing through the exit-posts and out of the compound. In their midst, unprotesting, was Leonards. He didn't look back, and Devall was glad of it.

THE COLONEL stared at the row of books a long time, the frayed spools that had followed him around from world to world, from gray Danelon to stormy Lurrin to bone-dry Korvel, and on to Hegath and M'Qualt and the others, and now to warm blue-skied Markin. Shaking his head, he turned away and dropped heavily into the foam cradle behind his desk.

He snapped on the autotype with a savage gesture and dictated a full account of his actions, from the very start until his climactic decision, and smiled bitterly. There would be a certain time-lag, but before long the autotype facsimile machine in the E-T Department's basement would start clacking, there in Rio, and Thornton would know what Devall had done.

And Thornton would be stuck with it as Department policy henceforth.

Devall switched on the intercom and said, "I'm not to be disturbed under any circumstances. If there's anything urgent, have it sent to Major Grey; he's acting head of the base until I countermand. And if any messages come from Earth let Grey have them too.

He wondered if they'd relieve him of his command immediately, or wait until he got back to Earth. The latter, more likely; Thornton had some subtlety, if not much. But there was certain to be an inquiry, and a head would roll.

Devall shrugged and stretched back. *I did what was right,* he told himself firmly. *That's the one thing I can be sure of.*

But I hope I don't ever have to face my sister again.

He dozed, after a while, eyes half-open and slipping rapidly closed. Sleep came to him, and he welcomed it, for he was terribly tired.

He was awakened suddenly, by a loud outcry. A jubilant shout from a dozen throats at once, splitting the afternoon calm. Devall felt a moment's disorientation; then, awakening rapidly, he sprang to the window and peered out.

A figure—alone and on foot—was coming through the open gateway. He wore regulation uniform, but it was dripping wet, and torn in several places. His blond hair was plastered to his scalp as if he had been swimming; he looked fatigued.

Leonards.

The colonel was nearly halfway out the front door before he realized that his uniform was in improper order. He forced himself back, tidied his clothing, and with steely dignity strode out the door a second time.

Leonards stood surrounded by a smiling knot of men, enlisted men and officers alike. The boy was grinning wearily.

"Attention!" Devall barked, and immediately the area fell silent. He stepped forward.

Leonards raised one arm in an exhausted salute. There were some ugly bruises on him.

"I'm back, Colonel."

"I'm aware of that. You understand that I'll have to return you to the Marks for trial anyway, despite your no doubt daring escape?"

The boy smiled and shook his head. "No, sir. You don't follow, sir. The trial's over. I've been tried and acquitted."

"What's that?"

"It was trial by ordeal, Colonel. They prayed for half an hour or so, and then they dumped me in the lake down the road. The dead man's two brothers came after me and tried to drown me, but I outswam them and came up safely on the other side."

He shook his hair like a drenched cat, scattering a spray of water several feet in the air. "They nearly had me, once. But as soon as I got across the lake alive and undrowned, it proved to them I couldn't have meant any harm. So they declared me innocent, apologized, and turned me loose. They were still praying when I left them."

There seemed to be no bitterness in Leonards' attitude; apparently, Devall thought, he had understood the reason for the decision to hand him over, and would not hold it against him now. That was gratifying.

"You'd better get to your quarters and dry off, Lieutenant. And then come to my office. I'd like to talk to you there."

"Yes, sir."

Devall spun sharply and headed back across the clearing to his office. He slammed the door behind him and switched on the autotype. The report to Earth would have to be amended now.

A moment or two after he had finished, the intercom glowed. He turned it on and heard Steber's voice saying, "Sir, the old priest is here. He wants to apologize to you for everything. He's wearing clothing of celebration, and he brought a peace-offering for us."

"Tell him I'll be right out," Devall said. "And call all the men together. Including Dudley. *Especially* Dudley. I want him to see this."

He slipped off his sweat-stained jacket and took a new one out. Surveying himself in the mirror, he nodded approvingly.

Well, well, he thought. *So the boy came through it safely. That's good.*

But he knew that the fate of Paul Leonards had been irrelevant all along, except on the sheerly personal level. It was the larger issue that counted.

For the first time, Earth had made a concrete demonstration of the equality-of-intelligent-life doctrine it had been preaching so long. He had shown that he respected the Markin laws in terms of what they were *to the Marks,* and he had won the affection of a race as a result. Having the boy return unharmed was a bonus.

But the precedent had been set. And the next time, perhaps, on some other world, the outcome might not be so pleasant. Some cultures had pretty nasty ways of putting criminals to death.

He realized that the burden the Earth exploration teams carried now had become many times heavier—that now, Earthmen would be subject to the laws of the planets who hosted them, and no more unwitting botanical excursions into sacred gardens could be tolerated. But it was for the ultimate good, he thought. We've shown them that we're not overlords, and that most of us don't want to be overlords. And now the thumb comes down on *us.*

He opened the door and stepped out. The men had gathered, and the old priest knelt abjectly at the foot of the steps, bearing some sort of enamelled box as his offering. Devall smiled and returned the bow, and lifted the old alien gently to his feet.

We'll have to be on our best behavior from now on, he thought. *We'll really have to watch our steps. But it'll be worth it.*

∞ ∞ ∞

NEVER MEET AGAIN

BY ALGIS BUDRYS

Never Meet Again

By Algis Budrys

Illustrated by Bill Bowman

THE BREEZE soughed through the linden trees. It was warm and gentle as it drifted along the boulevard. It tugged at the dresses of the girls strolling with their young men and stirred their modishly cut hair. It set the banners atop the government buildings to flapping, and it brought with it the sound of a jet aircraft—a Heinkel or a Messerschmitt—rising into the sky from Tempelhof Aerodrome. But when it touched Professor Kempfer on his bench it brought him only the scent of the Parisian perfumes and the sight of gaily colored frocks swaying around the girls' long, healthy legs.

Doctor Professor Kempfer straightened his exhausted shoulders and raised his heavy head. His deep, strained eyes struggled to break through their now habitual dull stare.

It was spring again, he realized in faint surprise. The pretty girls were eating their lunches hastily once more, so that they and their young men could stroll along *Unter Den Linden,* and the young men in the broad-shouldered jackets were clear-eyed and full of their own awakening strength.

And of course Professor Kempfer wore no overcoat today. He was not quite the comic pedant who wore his galoshes in the sunshine. It was only that he had forgotten, for the moment. The strain of these last few days had been very great.

All these months—these years—he had been doing his government-subsidized research and the other thing, too. Four or five hours for the government, and then a full day on the much more important thing no one knew about. Twelve, sixteen hours a day. Home to his very nice government apartment, where Frau Ritter, the housekeeper, had his supper ready. The supper eaten, to bed. And in the morning; cocoa, a bit of pastry, and to work. At noon he would leave his laboratory for a little while, to come here and eat the slice of black bread and cheese Frau Ritter had wrapped in waxed paper and put in his pocket before he left the house.

But it was over, now. Not the government sinecure—that was just made work for the old savant

He had spent fifteen patient years of painstaking work, all to construct an exit—which could be used only once!

who, after all, held the Knight's Cross of the Iron Cross for his work with the anti-submarine radar detector. That, of course, had been fifteen years ago. If they could not quite pension him off, still no one expected anything of a feeble old man puttering around the apparatus they had given him to play with.

And they were right, of course. Nothing *would* ever come of it. But the other thing . . .

That was done, now. After this last little rest he would go back to his laboratory in the *Himmlerstrasse* and take the final step. So now he could let himself relax and feel the warmth of the sun.

PROFESSOR KEMPFER smiled wearily at the sunshine. The good, constant sun, he thought, that gives of itself to all of us, no matter who or where we are. Spring . . . April, 1958.

Had it really been fifteen years —and sixteen years since the end of the war? It didn't seem possible. But then one day had been exactly like another for him, with only an electric light in the basement where his real apparatus was, an electric light that never told him whether it was morning, noon, or night.

I have become a cave-dweller! he thought with sudden realization. I have forgotten to think in terms of serial time. What an odd little trick I have played on myself!

Had he *really* been coming here, to this bench, every clear day for *fifteen* years? Impossible! But . . .

He counted on his fingers. 1940 was the year England had surrendered, with its air force destroyed and the Luftwaffe flying unchallenged air cover for the swift invasion. He had been sent to England late that year, to supervise the shipment home of the ultra-short wave-length radar from the Royal Navy's anti-submarine warfare school. And 1941 was the year the U-boats took firm control of the Atlantic. 1942 was the year the Russians lost at Stalingrad, starved by the millions, and surrendered to a Wehrmacht fed on shiploads of Argentinian beef. 1942 was the end of the war, yes.

So it *had* been that long.

I have become an indrawn old man, he thought to himself in bemusement. So very busy with myself . . . and the world has gone by, even while I sat here and might have watched it, if I'd taken the trouble. The world . . .

He took the sandwich from his coat pocket, unwrapped it, and began to eat. But after the first few bites he forgot it, and held it in one hand while he stared sightlessly in front of him.

His pale, mobile lips fell into a wry smile. The world—the vigorous young world, so full of strength, so confident . . . while I worked in my cellar like some Bolshevik dreaming of a fantastic bomb that would wipe out all my enemies at a stroke.

But what I have is not a bomb, and I have no enemies. I am an honored citizen of the greatest empire the world has ever known. Hitler is thirteen years dead in his auto accident, and the new chancellor is a different sort of man. He has promised us no war with the Americans. We have peace, and triumph, and these create a different sort of atmosphere than do war and desperation. We have relaxed, now. We have the fruit of our victory—what do we not have, in our empire of a thousand years? Western civilization is safe at last from the hordes of the East. Our future is assured. There is nothing, no one to fight, and these young people walking here have never known a moment's doubt, an instant's question of their place in an endlessly bright tomorrow. I will soon die, and the rest of us who knew the old days will die soon enough. It will all belong to the young people—all this eternal world. It belongs to them already. It is just that some of us old ones have not yet gotten altogether out of the way.

He stared out at the strolling crowds. How many years can I possibly have left to me? Three? Two? Four? I could die tomorrow.

He sat absolutely still for a moment, listening to the thick old blood slurring through his veins, to the thready flutter of his heart. It hurt his eyes to see. It hurt his throat to breathe. The skin of his hands was like spotted old paper.

Fifteen years of work. Fifteen years in his cellar, building what he had built—for what? Was his apparatus going to change anything? Would it detract even one trifle from this empire? Would it alter the life of even one citizen in that golden tomorrow?

This world would go on exactly as it was. Nothing would change in the least. So, what had he worked for? For himself? For this outworn husk of one man?

Seen in that light, he looked like a very stupid man. Stupid, foolish—monomaniacal.

Dear God, he thought with a rush of terrible intensity, am I now going to persuade myself not to use what I have built?

For all these years he had worked, worked—without stopping, without thinking. Now, in this first hour of rest, was he suddenly going to spit on it all?

A STOUT BULK settled on the bench beside him. "Jochim," the complacent voice said.

Professor Kempfer looked up. "Ah, Georg!" he said with an embarrassed laugh, "You startled me."

Doctor Professor Georg Tanzler guffawed heartily. "Oh, Jochim, Jochim!" he chuckled, shaking his head. "What a type you are! A thousand times I've found you here at noon, and each time it seems as if it surprises you. What do you think about, here on your bench?"

Professor Kempfer let his eyes stray. "Oh, I don't know," he said gently. "I look at the young people."

"The girls—" Tanzler's elbow dug roguishly into his side. "The girls, eh, Jochim?"

A veil drew over Professor Kempfer's eyes. "No," he whispered. "Not like that. No."

"What, then?"

"Nothing," Professor Kempfer said dully. "I look at nothing."

Tanzler's mood changed instantly. "So, he declared with precision. "I thought as much. Everyone knows you are working night and day, even though there is no need for it." Tanzler resurrected a chuckle. "We are not in any great hurry now. It's not as if we were pressed by anyone. The Australians and Canadians are fenced off by our navy. The Americans have their hands full in Asia. And your project, whatever it may be, will help no one if you kill yourself with overwork."

"You know there is no project," Professor Kempfer whispered. "You know it is all just busy work. No one reads my reports. No one checks my results. They give me the equipment I ask for, and do not mind, as long as it is not too much. You know that quite well. Why pretend otherwise?"

Tanzler sucked his lips. Then he shrugged. "Well, if you realize, then you realize," he said cheerfully. Then he changed expression again, and laid his hand on Professor Kempfer's arm in comradely fashion. "Jochim. It has been fifteen years. Must you still try to bury yourself?"

Sixteen, Professor Kempfer corrected, and then realized Tanzler was not thinking of the end of the war. Sixteen years since then, yes, but fifteen since Marthe died. Only fifteen?

I *must* learn to think in terms of serial time again. He realized

Tanzler was waiting for a response, and mustered a shrug.

"Jochim! Have you been listening to me?"

"Listening? Of course, Georg."

"Of course!" Tanzler snorted, his moustaches fluttering. "Jochim," he said positively, "it is not as if we were young men, I admit. But life goes on, even for us old crocks." Tanzler was a good five years Kempfer's junior. "We must look ahead—we must live for a future. We cannot let ourselves sink into the past. I realize you were very fond of Marthe. Every man is fond of his wife—that goes without saying. But fifteen years, Jochim! Surely, it is proper to grieve. But to *mourn*, like this—this is not *healthy!"*

One bright spark singed through the quiet barriers Professor Kempfer had thought perfect. "Were *you* ever in a camp, Georg?" he demanded, shaking with pent-up violence.

"A camp?" Tanzler was taken aback. "I? Of course not, Jochim! But—but you and Marthe were not in a real *lager*—it was just a . . . a . . . Well, you were under the State's protection! After all, Jochim!"

Professor Kempfer said stubbornly: "But Marthe *died*. Under the State's protection."

"These things *happen*, Jochim! After all, you're a reasonable man — Marthe — tuberculosis — even sulfa has its limitations—that might have happened to *anyone!"*

"She did not have tuberculosis in 1939, when we were placed under the State's protection. And when I finally said yes, I would go to work for them, and they gave me the radar detector to work on, they promised me it was only a little congestion in her bronchiae and that as soon as she was well they would bring her home. And the war ended, and they did *not* bring her home. I was given the Knight's Cross from Hitler's hands, personally, but they did *not* bring her home. And the last time I went to the sanitarium to see her, she was *dead*. And they paid for it all, and gave me my laboratory here, and an apartment, and clothes, and food, and a very good housekeeper, but Marthe was *dead."*

"Fifteen *years*, Jochim! Have you not forgiven us?"

"No. For a little while today —just a little while ago—I thought I might. But—no."

Tanzler puffed out his lips and fluttered them with an exhaled breath. "So," he said. "What are you going to do to us for it?"

Professor Kempfer shook his head. "To you? What should I do to you? The men who arranged these things are all dead, or dying. If I had some means of hurting the Reich—and I do not —how could I revenge myself on these children?" He looked toward the passersby. "What am I to them, or they to me? No—no, I am going to do nothing to you."

Tanzler raised his eyebrows and put his thick fingertips together. "If you are going to do nothing to us, then what are you going to do to yourself?"

"I am going to go away." Already, Professor Kempfer was ashamed of his outburst. He felt he had controverted his essential character. A man of science, after all—a thinking, *reasoning* man—could not let himself descend to emotional levels. Professor Kempfer was embarrassed to think that Tanzler might believe this sort of lapse was typical of him.

"Who am I," he tried to explain, "to be judge and jury over a whole nation—an empire? Who is one man, to decide good and evil? I look at these youngsters, and I envy them with all my heart. To be young; to find all the world arranged in orderly fashion for one's special benefit; to have been placed on a surfboard, free to ride the crest of the wave forever, and never to have to swim at all! Who am I, Georg? Who am I?

"But I do not like it here. So I am going away."

Tanzler looked at him enigmatically. "To Carlsbad. For the radium waters. Very healthful. We'll go together." He began pawing Professor Kempfer's arm with great heartiness. "A splendid idea! I'll get the seats reserved on the morning train. We'll have a holiday, eh, Jochim?"

"No!" He struggled to his feet, pulling Tanzler's hand away from his arm. *"No!"* He staggered when Tanzler gave way. He began to walk fast, faster than he had walked in years. He looked over his shoulder, and saw Tanzler lumbering after him.

He began to run. He raised an arm. "Taxi! *Taxi!"* He lurched toward the curb, while the strolling young people looked at him wide-eyed.

He hurried through the ground floor laboratory, his heart pumping wildly. His eyes were fixed on the plain gray door to the fire stairs, and he fumbled in his trousers pocket for the key. He stumbled against a bench and sent apparatus crashing over. At the door, he steadied himself and, using both hands, slipped the key into the lock. Once through the door, he slammed it shut and locked it again, and listened to the hoarse whistle of his breath in his nostrils.

Then, down the fire stairs he clattered, open-mouthed. Tanzler. Tanzler would be at a telephone, somewhere. Perhaps the State Police were out in the streets, in their cars, coming here, already.

He wrenched open the basement door, and locked it behind him in the darkness before he turned on the lights. With his chest aching, he braced himself on widespread feet and looked at the dull sheen of yellow light on the racks of gray metal cabinets. They rose about him like the blocks of a Mayan temple, with dials for carvings and pilot lights for jewels, and he moved down the narrow aisle between them, slowly and quietly now, like a last, enfeebled acolyte. As he walked he threw switches, and the cabinets began to resonate in chorus.

The aisle led him, irrevocably, to the focal point. He read what the dials on the master panel told him, and watched the power demand meter inch into the green.

If they think to open the building circuit breakers!

If they shoot through the door!

If I was wrong!

Now there were people hammering on the door. Desperately weary, he depressed the firing switch.

There was a galvanic thrum, half pain, half pleasure, as the vibratory rate of his body's atoms was changed by an infinitesimal degree. Then he stood in dank darkness, breathing musty air, while whatever parts of his equipment had been included in the field fell to the floor.

Behind him, he left nothing. Vital resistors had, by design, come with him. The overloaded apparatus in the basement laboratory began to stench and burn under the surge of full power, and to sputter in Georg Tanzler's face.

THE BASEMENT he was in was not identical with the one he had left. That could only mean that in this Berlin, something serious had happened to at least one building on the Himmlerstrasse. Professor Kempfer searched through the darkness with weary patience until he found a door, and while he searched he considered the thought that some upheaval, man-made or natural, had filled in the ground for dozens of meters above his head, leaving only this one pocket of emptiness into which his apparatus had shunted him.

When he finally found the door he leaned against it for some time, and then he gently eased it open. There was nothing but blackness on the other side, and at his first step he tripped and sprawled on a narrow flight of stairs, bruising a hip badly. He found his footing again. On quivering legs he climbed slowly and as silently as he could, clinging to the harsh, newly-sawed wood of the bannister. He could not seem to catch his breath. He had to gulp for air, and the darkness was shot through with red swirlings.

He reached the top of the stairs, and another door. There was harsh gray light seeping around it, and he listened intently, allowing for the quick suck and thud of the pulse in his ears. When he heard nothing for a long time, he opened it. He was at the end of a long corridor lined with doors, and at the end there was another door opening on the street.

Eager to get out of the building, and yet reluctant to leave as much as he knew of this world, he moved down the corridor with exaggerated caution.

It was a shoddy building. The paint on the walls was cheap, and the linoleum on the floor was scuffed and warped. There were cracks in the plastering. Everything was rough—half finished, with paint slapped over it, everything drab. There were numbers on the doors, and dirty rope mats in front of them. It was an apartment house, then—but from the way the doors were jammed almost against each other, the apartments had to be no more than cubicles.

Dreary, he thought. Dreary, dreary—who would live in such a place? Who would put up an apartment house for people of mediocre means in this neighborhood?

But when he reached the street, he saw that it was humpy and cobblestoned, the cobbling badly patched, and that all the buildings were like this one—gray-faced, hulking, ugly. There was not a building he recognized—not a stick or stone of the *Himmlerstrasse* with its fresh cement roadway and its sapling trees growing along the sidewalk. And yet he knew he must be on the exact spot where the *Himmlerstrasse* had been—was—and he could not quite understand.

He began to walk in the direction of *Unter Den Linden*. He was far from sure he could reach it on foot, in his condition, but he would pass through the most familiar parts of the city, and could perhaps get some inkling of what had happened.

HE HAD SUSPECTED that the probability world his apparatus could most easily adjust him for would be one in which Germany had lost the war. That was a large, dramatic difference, and though he had refined his work as well as he could, any first model of any equipment was bound to be relatively insensitive.

But as he walked along, he found himself chilled and repelled by what he saw.

Nothing was the same. Nothing. Even the layout of the streets had changed a little. There were new buildings everywhere—new buildings of a style and workmanship that had made them old in atmosphere the day they were completed. It was the kind of total reconstruction that he had no doubt the builders stubbornly proclaimed was "Good as New," because to say it was as good as the old Berlin would have been to invite bitter smiles.

The people in the streets were grim, gray-faced, and shoddy. They stared blankly at him and his suit, and once a dumpy woman carrying a string bag full of lumpy packages turned to her similar companion and muttered as he passed that he looked like an American with his extravagant clothes.

The phrase frightened him. What kind of war had it been, that there would still be Americans to be hated in Berlin in 1958? How long could it possibly have lasted, to account for so many old buildings gone? What had pounded Germany so cruelly? And yet even the "new" buildings were genuinely some years old. Why an American? Why not an Englishman or Frenchman?

He walked the gray streets, looking with a numb sense of settling shock at this grim Berlin. He saw men in shapeless uniform caps, brown trousers, cheap boots and sleazy blue shirts. They wore armbands with *Volkspolizei* printed on them. Some of them had not bothered to shave this morning or to dress in fresh uniforms. The civilians looked at them sidelong and then pretended not to have seen them. For an undefinable but well-remembered reason, Professor Kempfer slipped by them as inconspicuously as possible.

He grappled at what he saw with the dulled resources of his overtired intellect, but there was no point of reference with which to begin. He even wondered if perhaps the war was somehow still being fought, with unimaginable alliances and unthinkable antagonists, with all resources thrown into a brutal, dogged struggle from which all hope of both defeat and victory were gone, and only endless straining effort loomed up from the future.

Then he turned the corner and saw the stubby military car, and soldiers in baggy uniforms with red stars on their caps. They were parked under a weatherbeaten sign which read, in German above a few lines in unreadable Cyrillic characters: *Attention! You Are Leaving the U.S.S.R. Zone of Occupation. You Are Entering the American Zone of Occupation. Show Your Papers.*

God in heaven! he thought, recoiling. The Bolsheviks. And he was on their side of the line. He turned abruptly, but did not move for an instant. The skin of his face felt tight. Then he broke into a stumbling walk, back the way he had come.

He had not come into this world blindly. He had not dared bring any goods from his apartment, of course. Not with Frau Ritter to observe him. Nor had he expected that his Reichsmarks would be of any use. He had provided for this by wearing two diamond-set rings. He had expected to have to walk down to the jewelry district before he could begin to settle into this world, but he had expected no further difficulty.

He had expected Germany to have lost the war. Germany had lost another war within his lifetime, and fifteen years later it would have taken intense study for a man in his present position to detect it.

Professor Kempfer had thought it out, slowly, systematically. He had not thought that a Soviet checkpoint might lie between him and the jewelry district.

It was growing cold, as the afternoon settled down. It had not been as warm a day to begin with, he suspected, as it had been in his Berlin. He wondered how it might be, that Germany's losing a war could change the weather, but the important thing was that he was shivering. He was beginning to attract attention not only for his suit but for his lack of a coat.

He had now no place to go, no place to stay the night, no way of getting food. He had no papers, and no knowledge of where to get them or what sort of maneuver would be required to keep him safe from arrest. If anything could save him from arrest. By Russians.

Professor Kempfer began to walk with dragging steps, his body sagging and numb. More and more of the passersby were looking at him sharply. They might well have an instinct for a hunted man. He did not dare look at the occasional policeman.

He was an old man. He had run today, and shaken with nervous anticipation, and finished fifteen years' work, and it had all been a nightmarish error. He felt his heart begin to beat unnaturally in his ears, and he felt a leaping flutter begin in his chest. He stopped, and swayed, and then he forced himself to cross the sidewalk so he could lean against a building. He braced his back and bent his knees a little, and let his hands dangle at his sides.

The thought came to him that there was an escape for him into one more world. His shoulderblades scraped a few centimeters downward against the wall.

There were people watching him. They ringed him in at a distance of about two meters, looking at him with almost childish curiosity. But there was something about them that made Professor Kempfer wonder at the conditions that could produce such children. As he looked back at them, he thought that perhaps they all wanted to help him—that would account for their not going on about their business. But they did not know what sort of complications their help might bring to them—except that there would certainly be complications. So none of them approached him. They gathered around him, watching, in a crowd that would momentarily attract a *volkspolizier*.

He looked at them dumbly, breathing as well as he could, his palms flat against the wall. There were stocky old women, round-shouldered men, younger men with pinched faces, and young girls with an incalculable wisdom in their eyes. And there was a bird-like older woman, coming quickly along the sidewalk, glancing at him curiously, then hurrying by, skirting around the crowd. . . .

There was one possibility of his escape to this world that Professor Kempfer had not allowed himself to consider. He pushed himself away from the wall, scattering the crowd as though by physical force, and lurched toward the passing woman.

"Marthe!"

She whirled, her purse flying to the ground. Her hand went to her mouth. She whispered, through her knuckles: "Jochim . . . Jochim . . ." He clutched her, and they supported each other. "Jochim . . . the American bombers killed you in Hamburg . . . yesterday I sent money to put flowers on your grave . . . Jochim . . ."

"It was a mistake. It was all a mistake. Marthe . . . we have found each other . . ."

FROM A DISTANCE, she had not changed very much at all. Watching her move about the room as he lay, warm and clean, terribly tired, in her bed, he thought to himself that she had not aged half as much as he. But when she bent over him with the cup of hot soup in her hand, he saw the sharp lines in her face, around her eyes and mouth, and when she spoke he heard the dry note in her voice.

How many years? he thought. How many years of loneliness and grief? *When* had the Americans bombed Hamburg? How? What kind of aircraft could bomb Germany from bases in the Western Hemisphere?

They had so much to explain to each other. As she worked to make him comfortable, the questions flew between them.

"It was something I stumbled on. The theory of probability worlds—of alternate universes. Assuming that the characteristic would be a difference in atomic vibration—minute, you understand; almost infinitely minute—assuming that somewhere in the gross universe every possible variation of every event *must* take place—then if some means could be found to alter the vibratory rate within a field, then any object in that field would automatically become part of the universe corresponding to that vibratory rate. . . .

"Marthe, I can bore you later.

Tell me about *Hamburg*. Tell me how we lost the war. Tell me about Berlin."

He listened while she told him how their enemies had ringed them in—how the great white wastes of Russia had swallowed their men, and the British fire bombers had murdered children in the night. How the Wehrmacht fought, and fought, and smashed their enemies back time after time, until all the best soldiers were dead. And how the Americans, with their dollars, had poured out countless tons of equipment to make up for their inability to fight. How, at the last, the vulture fleets of bombers had rumbled inexhaustibly across the sky, killing, killing, killing, until all the German homes and German families had been destroyed. And how now the Americans, with their hellish bomb that had killed a hundred thousand Japanese civilians, now bestrode the world and tried to bully it, with their bombs and their dollars, into final submission.

How? Professor Kempfer thought. How could such a thing have happened?

Slowly, he pieced it together, mortified to find himself annoyed when Marthe interrupted with constant questions about his Berlin and especially about his equipment.

And, pieced together, it still refused to seem logical.

How could anyone believe that Goering, in the face of all good sense, would turn the Luftwaffe from destroying the R.A.F. bases to a ridiculous attack on English cities? How could anyone believe that German electronics scientists could persistently refuse to believe ultra-shortwave radar was practical—refuse to believe it even when the Allied hunter planes were finding surfaced submarines at night with terrible accuracy?

What kind of nightmare world was this, with Germany divided and the Russians in control of Europe, in control of Asia, reaching for the Middle East that no Russian, not even the dreaming czars, had seriously expected ever to attain?

"Marthe—we must get out of this place. We must. I will have to rebuild my machine." It would be incredibly difficult. Working clandestinely as he must, scraping components together—even now that the work had been done once, it would take several years.

Professor Kempfer looked inside himself to find the strength he would need. And it was not there. It simply was gone, used up, burnt out, eaten out.

"Marthe, you will have to help me. I must take some of your strength. I will need so many things—identity papers, some kind of work so we can eat, money to buy equipment. . . ." His voice trailed away. It was so much, and there was so little time left for him. Yet, somehow, they must do it.

A hopelessness, a feeling of inevitable defeat, came over him. It was this world. It was poisoning him.

Marthe's hand touched his brow. "Hush, Jochim. Go to sleep. Don't worry. Everything is all right, now. My poor Jochim, how terrible you look! But everything will be all right. I must go back to work, now. I am hours late already. I will come back as soon as I can. Go to sleep, Jochim."

He let his breath out in a long, tired sigh. He reached up and touched her hand. "Marthe . . ."

HE AWOKE to Marthe's soft urging. Before he opened his eyes he had taken her hand from his shoulder and clasped it tightly. Marthe let the contact linger for a moment, then broke it gently.

"Jochim—my superior at the Ministry is here to see you."

He opened his eyes and sat up. "Who?"

"Colonel Lubintsev, from the People's Government Ministerium, where I work. He would like to speak to you." She touched him reassuringly. "Don't worry. It's all right. I spoke to him—I explained. He's not here to arrest you. He's waiting in the other room."

He looked at Marthe dumbly. "I—I must get dressed," he managed to say after a while.

"No—no, he wants you to stay in bed. He knows you're exhausted. He asked me to assure you it would be all right. Rest in bed. I'll get him."

Professor Kempfer sank back. He looked unseeingly up at the ceiling until he heard the sound of a chair being drawn up beside him, and then he slowly turned his head.

Colonel Lubintsev was a stocky, ruddy-faced man with gray bristles on his scalp. He had an astonishingly boyish smile. "Doctor Professor Kempfer, I am honored to meet you," he said. "Lubinstev, Colonel, assigned as advisor to the People's Government Ministerium." He extended his hand gravely, and Professor Kempfer shook it with a conscious effort.

"I am pleased to make your acquaintance," Professor Kempfer mumbled.

"Not at all, Doctor Professor. Not at all. Do you mind if I smoke?"

"Please." He watched the colonel touch a lighter to a long cigarette while Marthe quickly found a saucer for an ashtray. The colonel nodded his thanks to Marthe, puffed on the cigarette, and addressed himself to Professor Kempfer while Marthe sat down on a chair against the far wall.

"I have inspected your dossier," Colonel Lubintsev said. "That is," with a smile, "our dossier on your late counterpart. I see you fit the photographs as well as could be expected. We will have to make a further identification, of course, but I rather think that will be a formality." He smiled again. "I am fully prepared to accept your story. It is too fantastic not to be true. Of course, sometimes foreign agents choose their cover stories with that idea in mind, but not in this case, I think. If what has happened to you could happen to any man, our dossier indicates Jochim Kempfer might well be that man." Again, the smile. "In any counterpart."

"You have a dossier," Professor Kempfer said.

Colonel Lubintsev's eyebrows went up in a pleased grin. "Oh, yes. When we liberated your nation, we knew exactly what scientists were deserving of our assistance in their work, and where to find them. We had laboratories, project agendas, living quarters—everything!—all ready for them. But I must admit, we did not think we would ever be able to accommodate you."

"But now you can."

"Yes!" Once more, Colonel Lubintsev smiled like a little boy with great fun in store. "The possibilities of your device are as infinite as the universe! Think of the enormous help to the people of your nation, for example, if they could draw on machine tools and equipment from such alternate places as the one you have just left." Colonel Lubintsev waved his cigarette. "Or if, when the Americans attack us, we can transport bombs from a world where the revolution is an accomplished fact, and have them appear in North America in this."

Professor Kempfer sat up in bed. "Marthe! Marthe, why have you done this to me?"

"Hush, Jochim," she said. "Please. Don't tire yourself. I have done nothing to you. You will have care, now. We will be able to live together in a nice villa, and you will be able to work, and we will be together."

"Marthe—"

She shook her head, her lips pursed primly. "Please, Jochim. Times have changed a great deal, here. I explained to the Colonel that your head was probably still full of the old Nazi propaganda. He understands. You will learn to see it for what it was. And you will help put the Americans back in their place." Her eyes filled suddenly with tears. "All the years I went to visit your grave as often as I could. All the years I paid for flowers, and all the nights I cried for you."

"But I am *here*, Marthe! I am here! I am not dead."

"Jochim, Jochim," she said gently. "Am I to have had all my grief for nothing?"

"I have brought a technical expert with me," Colonel Lubintsev went on as though nothing had happened. "If you will tell him what facilities you will need, we can begin preliminary work immediately." He rose to his feet. "I will send him in. I myself must be going." He put out his cigarette, and extended his hand. "I have been honored, Doctor Professor Kempfer."

"Yes," Professor Kempfer whispered. "Yes. Honored." He raised his hand, pushed it toward the colonel's, but could not hold it up long enough to reach. It fell back to the coverlet, woodenly, and Professor Kempfer could not find the strength to move it. "Goodbye."

He heard the colonel walk out with a few murmured words for Marthe. He was quite tired, and he heard only a sort of hum.

He turned his head when the technical expert came in. The man was all eagerness, all enthusiasm:

"Jochim! This is amazing! Perhaps I should introduce myself—I worked with your counterpart during the war—we were quite good friends—I am Georg Tanzler. Jochim! How *are* you!"

Professor Kempfer looked up. His lips twisted. "I think I am going away again, Georg," he whispered.

∞ ∞ ∞

TALES FOR TOMORROW

No shortage here.... The April issue of INFINITY will, in fact, relieve the current shortage of two items that are much in demand: *One*: Clifford D. Simak, never around as much as most of us would like, will be present with a long novelet entitled "Leg. Forst."—and what the title means is one of the pleasant surprises. This is a light-hearted, easy-going tale of a future hobbyist and the unexpected fruits of his avocation, with a dash of bitters blended smoothly into the effervescence of high spirits to make a heady draught.

Two: John Bernard Daley, who hasn't appeared since his "The Man Who Liked Lions" won immediate applause and enthusiastic devotees well over a year ago, will be back with a shorter novelet, "Wings of the Phoenix." This is a genuine science-fiction horror story, carrying pessimistically realistic extrapolation to a logical extreme and still managing to remain highly entertaining throughout.

Plus, of course, top-notch short stories and features.

THE LEAF

By ROBERT F. YOUNG

Even his present desperate situation couldn't spoil his memories of other days in the woods: like the lovely, lazy day he shot eleven squirrels....

Illustrated by RICHARD KLUGA

HE COULD REMEMBER the afternoon as if it were yesterday. It wasn't, of course—actually it had been several years back. It had been around the middle of autumn, about the time when the last incarnadine leaves were making their fluttering journeys earthward. He had taken his .22 and gone into the woods where the hickory trees were, and he had settled himself comfortably against the shaggy trunk of one of the hickories, the .22 balanced across his sprawled knees. Then he had waited.

The first red squirrel had come out on one of the high limbs and posed there. That was the word all right—posed. It had sat there on its haunches with utter immobility almost as if it had been painted on canvas against a background of leafless naked branches and milk-blue sky.

He had raised the .22 lazily and sighted along the slender barrel. There was no hurry. There was all the time in the world. He didn't squeeze the trigger until he had a perfect right-between-the-eyes bead, then he squeezed it ever so lightly. There was the sharp sound of the report, and then the small body falling swiftly, bouncing and glancing off limbs, tumbling over and over, making a rustling thump in the dry leaves at the tree's base.

He hadn't even bothered to go

over and examine it. He knew he'd got it right where he'd aimed. They didn't die instantly like that unless you got them in a vital spot. They thrashed and kicked around after they hit the ground and sometimes you had to waste another shell on them if the noise bothered you. Of course if the noise didn't bother you, you could save the shell for the next one, but it was better in the long run to get them right between the eyes because that way the others wouldn't be frightened away by the thrashing sound, and you didn't have to get up.

That had been the first one.

The second one had been coming down the trunk of the same tree, spiraling the trunk, the way squirrels do, stopping at frequent intervals and studying their surroundings with their bright beebees of eyes, looking right at you sometimes but never seeing you unless you moved. This one had stopped, head down, and was looking off to one side when he got it. The force of the bullet, striking just below the ear, where he'd aimed, tore the small red body right off the trunk, spun it around several times, and dropped it into a wild blackberry thicket.

He hadn't bothered to look at that one either. He had lit a cigarette and leaned back more comfortably against the hickory. It was a pleasant afternoon, mild for November—a time for wandering in woods, a time to take it a little easy, a time to knock off some of the scavengers and pests you'd neglected during the first days of pheasant and rabbit season, a time to get your eyes down to hair-line fineness for the first ecstatic day of deer. Red squirrels were easy, of course, a little beneath the dignity of a true hunter, but when you tried to bore them in vital spots you got some pretty good practice out of it.

He yawned. Then, out of the corner of his eye, he caught a red wisp of movement high in the tree to his right. He brought the .22 over casually. He hardly needed to turn his body at all. The stock fitted his shoulder snugly, lay cool against his cheek. There was no recoil, only the sharp ripping sound, and then the dark red body falling, hitting limbs, caroming, dropping, dropping, making the familiar thrilling rustling sound in the dead leaves.

That had been the third.

The fourth and the fifth had been about the same.

After the fifth, he had become a little bored. He decided to vary the game a little. He drew his knees together and rested the barrel of the .22 in the niche between them, then sat there quietly for a long time.

Presently the sixth squirrel left

the security of the trees and made a few quick jumps into the small clearing. Then it stopped and stood poised, a statuette except for its alive bright eyes. It was a perfect target, but he was in no hurry. He was enjoying himself immensely.

After about half a minute the squirrel moved again—several yards closer, almost in an exact line with the dark little eye of the .22. It sat up on its haunches then, its tail an arched question mark behind it. It put its tiny forepaws together and sat there not moving, almost as though it were praying. (That was the part he remembered most vividly.)

He'd hardly needed to move the .22 at all. The slightest shift had aligned the sights with the imaginary mark between the little eyes. He had squeezed the trigger nonchalantly, and the part of the head just above the eyes had come right off and the small red body had completed a perfect somersault before dropping into the dead leaves of the clearing.

After that he hadn't bothered with the trees. It was so much more fun in the clearing, waiting for them to come right up to you and pose. Of course it wasn't such good practice, but it was fine entertainment—an ideal way to spend a lazy afternoon in fall when the wood was all cut for winter, the crops in, the barn roof repaired and Pa off to town where he couldn't be finding annoying little things for you to do.

He had got eleven of them altogether, he hadn't missed a one, and he had felt pretty proud taking them home to show to Ma before feeding them to the dogs.

HE SHIFTED his cramped legs and peered down through the interstices of the foliage at the gray shape of the hunter. Some of his initial terror had left him when he'd finally realized that they couldn't see through leaves any more than he could; that They, as well as he, needed an open target in order to make a kill.

So he was relatively safe in the tree—for a while, at least. Perhaps he could find safety in trees for the rest of his life. Trees might be the answer.

He felt a little better. A portion of the fear that had followed the meteor shower was still with him, however. The fear that had detonated in his mind the morning after the shower when Pa had come running to the barn, shouting: "The cities! All the cities have been blowed up! They ain't no more cities in the whole world. Radio just said so 'fore it went dead. We're bein' invaded!"

Invaded? Invaded by whom? He hadn't been able to grasp it at first. At first he'd thought

Russia, and then he'd thought, no, it couldn't be Russia. Pa had said *all* the cities. All the cities in the whole wide world.

And then he'd begun to see the people on the road. The terrified people, the walking, running, stumbling people heading for the hills—the hills and the forests, the hiding places that ships couldn't see, that bombs couldn't find.

But that hunters could.

Hunters hunting with incredible silver guns, skimming along the roads to the hills and the forests in fantastic vehicles, alighting by roadsides and lumbering across fields to timber stands; routing out the people from elms and oaks and maples and locusts and even sumac, flushing them out like rabbits and shooting them down in cold blood with blinding shards of bullets.

He had run when he'd seen the first vehicle. He'd run wildly for the woods. He'd forgotten Pa and Ma. He'd even forgotten his gun. He'd been scared. Crazy-scared.

What did They want to kill people for? What was wrong with people?

He shivered on the limb, in the chill morning wind that had sprung up after the first frost of the season. Martians, he'd bet. Martians landing on Earth and wanting everything for Themselves, afraid to let people live for fear *they'd* get some. Greedy Martians, trying to hog the whole world!

The gray shape below him moved slightly and his terror broke out afresh. The hunter appeared to be reclining against the trunk of a nearby tree, its gleaming weapon resting on its huge tentacular legs. Waiting. For an irrational moment he considered climbing down and approaching it, getting down on his knees and begging it for mercy.

But he'd only be wasting his time. He realized that right away. He knew he'd see no pity in those cold inhuman eyes. He knew he'd see nothing but death.

The trees were the only answer. The trees with their friendly screens of foliage, their lofty leafy hiding places. By living in the trees a shrewd man might be able to elude the hunters forever. If he was careful. If he never let himself be seen.

He peered cautiously down at the hunter again. He looked at the gray patches of the gargantuan body that showed through the interstices of the foliage.

As he watched, the first frost-nipped leaf fluttered down past his face, hovering for a moment before his eyes so that he could not miss its new autumnal coloring.

∞ ∞ ∞

Accept No Substitutes

By ROBERT SHECKLEY

RALPH GARVEY's private space yacht was in the sling at Boston Spaceport, ready for takeoff. He was on yellow stand-by, waiting for the green, when his radio crackled.

"Tower to G43221," the radio buzzed. "Please await customs inspection."

"Righto," said Garvey, with a calmness he did not feel. Within him, something rolled over and died.

Customs inspection! Of all the black, accursed, triple-distilled bad luck! There was no regular inspection of small private yachts. The Department had its hands full with the big interstellar liners from Cassiopeia, Algol, Deneb, and a thousand other places. Private ships just weren't worth the time and money. But to keep them in line, Customs held occasional spot checks. No one knew when the mobile customs team would descend upon any particular spaceport. But chances of being inspected at any one time were less than fifty to one.

Garvey had been counting on that factor. And he had paid eight hundred dollars to know for certain that the East coast team was in Georgia. Otherwise, he would never have risked a twenty-year jail sentence for violation of the Sexual Morality Act.

There was a loud rap on his port. "Open for inspection, please."

"Righto," Garvey called out. He locked the door to the after-cabin. If the inspector wanted to

The Sexual Morality Act was fierce to buck, but the Algolian sex surrogate was . . . er . . . even fiercer!

Illustrated by ED EMSH

look there, he was sunk. There was no place in the ship where he could successfully conceal a packing case ten feet high, and no way he could dispose of its illegal contents.

"I'm coming," Garvey shouted. Beads of perspiration stood out on his high, pale forehead. He thought wildly of blasting off anyhow, running for it, to Mars, Venus. . . . But the patrol ships would get him before he had covered a million miles. There was nothing he could do but try to bluff it.

He touched a button. The hatch slid back and a tall, thin uniformed man entered.

"Thought you'd get away with it, eh, Garvey?" the inspector barked. "You rich guys never learn!"

Somehow, they had found out! Garvey thought of the packing crate in the after cabin, and its human-shaped, not-yet-living contents. Damning, absolutely damning. What a fool he'd been!

HE TURNED back to the control panel. Hanging from a corner of it, in a cracked leather holster, was his revolver. Rather than face twenty years breaking pumice on Lunar, he would shoot, then try—

"The Sexual Morality Act isn't a blue law, Garvey," the inspector continued, in a voice like steel against flint. "Violations can have a catastrophic effect upon the individual, to say nothing of the race. That's why we're going to make an example of you, Garvey. Now let's see the evidence."

"I don't know what in hell you're talking about," Garvey said. Surreptitiously his hand began to creep toward the revolver.

"Wake up, boy!" said the inspector. "You mean you *still* don't recognize me?"

Garvey stared at the inspector's tanned, humorous face. He said, "Eddie Starbuck?"

"About time! How long's it been, Ralph? Ten years?"

"At least ten," Garvey said. His knees were beginning to shake from sheer relief. "Sit down, sit down, Eddie! You still drink bourbon?"

"I'll say." Starbuck sat down on one of Garvey's acceleration couches. He looked around, and nodded.

"Nice. Very nice. You must be rich indeed, old buddy."

"I get by," Garvey said. He handed Starbuck a drink, and poured one for himself. They talked for a while about old times at Michigan State.

"And now you're a Customs inspector," Garvey said.

"Yeah," said Starbuck, stretching his long legs. "Always had a yen for the law. But it doesn't pay like transistors, eh?"

Garvey smiled modestly. "But what's all this about the Sexual

Morality Act? A gag?"

"Not at all. Didn't you hear the news this morning? The FBI found an underground sex factory. They hadn't been in business long, so it was possible to recover all the surrogates. All except one."

"Oh?" said Garvey, draining his drink.

"Yeah. That's when they called us in. We're covering all spaceports, on the chance the receiver will try to take the damned thing off Earth."

Garvey poured another drink and said, very casually, "So you figured I was the boy, eh?"

Starbuck stared at him a moment, then exploded into laughter. "You, Ralph? Hell, no! Saw your name on the spaceport out-list. I just dropped in for a drink, boy, for old time's sake. Listen, Ralph, I *remember* you. Hell-on-the-girls-Garvey. Biggest menace to virginity in the history of Michigan State. What would a guy like you want a substitute for?"

"My girls wouldn't stand for it," Garvey said, and Starbuck laughed again, and stood up.

"Look, I gotta run. Call me when you get back?"

"I sure will!" A little light-headed, he said, "Sure you don't want to inspect anyhow, as long as you're here?"

Starbuck stopped and considered. "I suppose I should, for the record. But to hell with it, I won't hold you up." He walked to the port, then turned. "You know, I feel sorry for the guy who's got that surrogate."

"Eh? Why?"

"Man, those things are poison! You know that, Ralph! Anything's possible—insanity, deformation. . . . And this guy may have even more of a problem."

"Why?"

"Can't tell you, boy," Starbuck said. "Really can't. It's special information. The FBI isn't certain yet. Besides, they're waiting for the right moment to spring it."

With an easy wave, Starbuck left. Garvey stared after him, thinking hard. He didn't like the way things were going. What had started out as an illicit little vacation was turning into a full-scale criminal affair. Why hadn't he thought of this earlier? He had been apprehensive in the sexual substitute factory, with its low lights, its furtive, white-aproned men, its reek of raw flesh and plastic. Why hadn't he given up the idea then? The surrogates couldn't be as good as people said. . . .

"Tower to G43221," the radio crackled. "Are you ready?"

Garvey hesitated, wishing he knew what Starbuck had been hinting at. Maybe he should stop now, while there was still time.

Then he thought of the giant crate in the after cabin, and its contents, waiting for activation, waiting for him. His pulse began to race. He knew that he was going through with it, no matter what the risk.

He signalled to the tower, and strapped himself into the control chair.

An hour later he was in space.

TWELVE HOURS later, Garvey cut his jets. He was a long way from Earth, but nowhere near Luna. His detectors, pushed to their utmost limit, showed nothing in his vicinity. No liners were going by, no freighters, no police ships, no yachts. He was alone. Nothing and no one was going to disturb him.

He went into the after cabin. The packing case was just as he had left it, securely fastened to the deck. Even the sight of it was vaguely exciting. Garvey pressed the activating stud on the outside of the case, and sat down to wait for the contents to awaken and come to life.

THE SURROGATES had been developed earlier in the century. They had come about from sheer necessity. At that time, mankind was beginning to push out into the galaxy. Bases had been established on Venus, Mars and Titan, and the first interstellar ships were arriving at Algol and Stagoe II. Man was leaving Earth.

Man—but not woman.

The first settlements were barely toeholds in alien environments. The work was harsh and demanding, and life expectancy was short. Whole settlements were sometimes wiped out before the ships were fully unloaded. The early pioneers were like soldiers on the line of battle, and exposed to risks no soldier had ever encountered.

Later there would be a place for women. Later—but not now.

So here and there, light-years from Earth, were little worlds without women—and not happy about it.

The men grew sullen, quarrelsome, violent. They grew careless, and carelessness on an alien planet was usually fatal.

They wanted women.

Since real women could not go to them, scientists on Earth developed substitutes. Android females were developed, the surrogates, and shipped to the colonies. It was a violation of Earth's morals; but there were worse violations on the way if these weren't accepted.

For a while, everything seemed to be fine. It would probably have gone on that way, had everyone left well enough alone.

But the companies on Earth had the usual desire to improve their product. They called in sculptors and artists to dress up the appearance of the package. Engineers tinkered with the surrogates, rewired them, built in subtler stimulus-response mechanisms, did strange things with conditioned reflexes. And the men of the settlements were very happy with the results.

So happy, in fact, that they refused to return to human women, even when they had the opportunity.

They came back to Earth after their tours of duty, these pioneers, and they brought their surrogates with them. Loud and long they praised the substitute women, and pointed out their obvious superiority to neurotic, nervous, frigid human women.

Naturally, other men wanted to try out the surrogates. And when they did, they were pleasantly surprised. And spread the word. And—

The government stepped in, quickly and firmly. For one thing, over fifty percent of the votes were at stake. But more important, social scientists predicted a violent drop in the birth rate if this went on. So the government destroyed the surrogates, outlawed the factories, and told everyone to return to normal.

And reluctantly, everyone did. But there were always some men who remembered, and told other men. And there were always some men who weren't satisfied with second-best. So . . .

GARVEY heard movements within the crate. He smiled to himself, remembering stories he had heard of the surrogates' piquant habits. Suddenly there was a high-pitched clanging. It was the standby alarm from the control room. He hurried forward.

It was an emergency broadcast, on all frequencies, directed to Earth and all ships at space. Garvey tuned it in.

"This is Edward Danzer," the radio announced crisply. "I am Chief of the Washington branch of the Federal Bureau of Investigation. You have all heard, on your local newscasts, of the detection and closure of an illegal sexual substitute factory. And you know that all except one of the surrogates have been found. This message is for the man who has that last surrogate, wherever he may be."

Garvey licked his lips nervously and hunched close to the radio. Within the after cabin, the surrogate was still making waking-up noises.

"That man is in danger!" Danzer said. "Serious danger! Our investigation of the molds and forms used in the factory showed us that something strange was going on. Just this morning, one of the factory technicians finally confessed.

"The missing surrogate is not an Earth model!

"I repeat," Danzer barked, "the missing surrogate is *not an Earth model!* The factory operators had been filling orders for the planet Algol IV. When they ran short of Earth models for humans, they substituted an Algolian model. Since the sale of a surrogate is illegal anyhow, they figured the customer would have no kickback."

Garvey sighed with relief. He had been afraid he had a small dinosaur in the packing case, at the very least.

"Perhaps," Danzer continued, "the holder of the Algolian surrogate does not appreciate his danger yet. It is true, of course, that the Algolians are of the species *homo sapiens*. It has been established that the two races share a common ancestry in the primeval past. But Algol is different from our Earth.

"The planet Algol IV is considerably heavier than Earth, and has a richer oxygen atmosphere. The Algolians, raised in this physical environment, have a markedly superior musculature to that of the typical Earthman. Colloquially, they are strong as rhinos.

"But the surrogate, of course, does not know this. She has a powerful and indiscriminate mating drive. *That's where the danger lies!* So I say to the customer—give yourself up now, while there's still time. And remember: crime does not pay."

The radio crackled static, then hummed steadily. Garvey turned it off. He had been taken, but good! He really should have inspected his merchandise before accepting it. But the crate had been sealed.

He was out a very nice chunk of money.

But, he reminded himself, he had lots of money. It was fortunate he had discovered the error in time. Now he would jettison the crate in space, and return to Earth. Perhaps real girls were best, after all. . . .

He heard the sound of heavy blows coming from the crate in the after cabin.

"I guess I'd better take care of you, honey," Garvey said, and walked quickly to the cabin.

A fusillade of blows rocked the crate. Garvey frowned and reached for the de-activating switch. As he did so, one side of the heavy crate splintered. Through the opening shot a long golden arm. The arm flailed wildly, and Garvey moved out of its way.

The situation wasn't humorous any more, he decided. The case rocked and trembled under the impact of powerful blows. Garvey estimated the force behind those blows, and shuddered. This had to be stopped at once. He ran toward the crate.

Long, tapered fingers caught his sleeve, ripping it off. Garvey managed to depress the de-activating stud and throw himself out of range.

There was a moment of silence. Then the surrogate delivered two blows with the impact of a pile driver. An entire side of the packing case splintered.

It was too late for de-activation.

GARVEY backed away. He was beginning to grow alarmed. The Algolian sexual substitute was preposterously strong; that seemed to be how they liked them on Algol. What passed for a tender love embrace on Algol would probably fracture the ribs of an Earthman. Not a nice outlook.

But wasn't it likely that the surrogate had some sort of discriminatory sense built in? Surely she must be able to differentiate between an Earthman and an Algolian. Surely . . .

The packing case fell apart, and the surrogate emerged.

She was almost seven feet tall, and gloriously, deliciously constructed. Her skin was a light golden-red, and her shoulder-length hair was lustrous black. Standing motionless, she looked to Garvey like a heroic statue of ideal femininity.

The surrogate was unbelievably beautiful—

And more dangerous than a cobra, Garvey reminded himself reluctantly.

"Well there," Garvey said, gazing up at her, "as you can see, a mistake has been made."

The surrogate stared at him with eyes of deepest gray.

"Yes ma'am," Garvey said, with a nervous little laugh, "it's really a ridiculous error. You, my dear, are an Algolian. I am an Earthman. We have nothing in common. Understand?"

Her red mouth began to quiver.

"Let me explain," Garvey went on. "You and I are from different races. That's not to say I consider you ugly. Quite the contrary! But unfortunately, there can never be anything between us, miss."

She looked at him uncomprehendingly.

"Never," Garvey repeated. He looked at the shattered packing case. "You don't know your own strength. You'd probably kill me inadvertently. And we wouldn't want that, would we?"

The surrogate murmured something deep in her beautiful throat.

"So that's the way it is," Garvey said briskly. "You stay right here, old girl. I'm going to the control room. We'll land on Earth in a few hours. Then I'll arrange to have you shipped to Algol. The boys'll really go for you on Algol! Sounds good, huh?"

The surrogate gave no sign of understanding. Garvey moved away. The surrogate pushed back her long hair and began to move toward him. Her intentions were unmistakeable.

Garvey backed away, step by step. He noticed that the surrogate was beginning to breathe heavily. Panic overtook him then, and he sprinted through the cabin door, slamming it behind him. The surrogate smashed against the door, calling to him in a clear, wordless voice. Garvey went to the instrument panel and began to evacuate the air from the after cabin.

Dial hands began to swing. Garvey heaved a sigh of relief and collapsed into a chair. It had been a close thing. He didn't like to think what would have happened if the Algolian sexual substitute had managed to seize him. Probably he would not have lived through the experience. He felt sorry at the necessity of killing so magnificent a creature, but it was the only safe thing to do.

He lighted a cigarette. As soon as she was dead, he would jettison her, crate and all, into space. Then he would get good and drunk. And at last, he would return to Earth a sadder and wiser man. No more substitutes for him! Plain, old-fashioned girls were good enough. Yessir, Garvey told himself, if women were all right for my father, they're all right for me. And when I have a son, I'm going to say to him, son, stick with women. They're all right. Accept no substitutes. Insist upon the genuine article. . . .

He was getting giddy, Garvey noticed. And his cigarette had gone out. He resisted a tremendous desire to giggle, and looked at his gauges. The air was leaving the after cabin, all right. But it was also leaving the control room.

Garvey sprang to his feet and inspected the cabin door. He swore angrily. That damned surrogate had managed to spring the hinges. The door was no longer airtight.

He turned quickly to the control board and stopped the evacuation of air. Why, he asked himself, did everything have to happen to him?

The surrogate renewed her battering tactics. She had picked up a metal chair and was hammering at the hinges.

But she couldn't break through a tempered-steel door, Garvey told himself. Oh, no. Not a chance. Never.

The door began to bulge ominously.

Garvey stood in the center of the control room, sweat rolling down his face, trying desperately to think. He could put on a spacesuit, then evacuate all the air from the ship. . . .

But the spacesuits, together with the rest of his equipment, were in the after cabin.

What else? This is serious, Garvey told himself. This is very serious. His mind seemed paralyzed. What could he do? Raise the temperature? Lower it?

He didn't know what the surrogate could stand. But he had a suspicion it was more than he could take.

One hinge shattered. The door bent, revealing the surrogate behind it, pounding relentlessly, her satiny skin glistening with perspiration.

Then Garvey remembered his revolver. He snatched it out of its holster and flipped off the safeties, just as the last hinge cracked and the door flew open.

"Stay in there," Garvey said, pointing the revolver.

The Algolian substitute moaned, and held out her arms to him. She smiled dazzlingly, seductively, and advanced upon him.

"Not another step!" Garvey shrieked, torn between fear and desire. He took aim, wondering if a bullet would stop her. . . .

And what would happen if it didn't.

The surrogate, her eyes blazing with passion, leaped for him. Garvey gripped the revolver in both shaking hands and began shooting. The noise was deafening. He fired three times, and the surrogate kept on coming.

"Stop!" Garvey screamed. "Please stop!"

Slower now, the surrogate advanced.

Garvey fired his fourth shot. Limping now, the surrogate came on, her desire unchecked.

Garvey backed to the wall. All he wanted now was to live long enough to get his hands on the factory operator. The surrogate gathered herself and pounced.

At point-blank range, Garvey fired his last shot.

THREE DAYS later, Garvey's ship received clearance and came down at Boston Spaceport. The landing was not made with Garvey's usual skill. On the final approach he scored a ten-foot hole in the reinforced concrete landing pit, but finally came to rest.

Eddie Starbuck hurried out to the ship and banged on the port. "Ralph! Ralph!"

Slowly the port swung open.

"Ralph! What in hell happened to you?" Starbuck cried.

Garvey looked as though he had been wrestling with a meat grinder and come out second-best. His face was bruised, and his hair had been badly scorched. He walked out of the ship with a pronounced limp.

"A power line overloaded," Garvey said. "Had quite a tussle before I could put everything out."

"Wow!" Starbuck said. "Look, Ralph, I'm sorry to put you through this now, but—well—"

"What's up?"

"Well, that damned surrogate still hasn't been found. The FBI has ordered inspection of all ships, private and commercial. I'm sorry to ask it now, after all you've been through—"

"Go right ahead," Garvey said.

The inspection was brief but thorough. Starbuck came out and checked his list.

"Thanks, Ralph. Sorry to bother you. That power line sure kicked up a mess, huh?"

"It did," Garvey said. "But I was able to jettison the furniture before it smoked me out. Now you'll have to excuse me, Eddie. I've got some unfinished business."

He started to walk away. Starbuck followed him.

"Look, boy, you'd better see a doctor. You aren't looking so good."

"I'm fine," Garvey said, his face set in an expression of implacable resolve.

Starbuck scratched his head and walked slowly to the control tower.

GARVEY caught a heli outside the spaceport. His head was beginning to ache again, and his legs were shaky.

The surrogate's strength and tenacity had been unbelievable. If she had been operating at her full capacity, he would never have survived. But that last shot at point-blank range had done it. No organism was constructed to take punishment like that. Not for very long.

He reached his destination in the center of Boston and paid off the heli. He was still very weak, but resolutely he marched across the street and entered a plain graystone building. His legs wobbled under him, and he thought again how fortunate he was to have gotten the surrogate.

Of course, the surrogate, with her amazing vitality, had also gotten him.

It had been brief—

But unforgettable.

He had been damned lucky to live through it. But it was his own fault for using substitutes.

A clerk hurried up to him. "Sorry to keep you waiting, sir. Can I help?"

"You can. I want passage to Algol, on the first ship leaving."

"Yes, sir. Round trip, sir?"

Garvey thought of the tall, glorious, black-haired, golden-skinned women he would find on Algol. Not substitutes this time, the real thing, with the all-important sense of judgment.

"One way," said Ralph Garvey, with a little smile of anticipation.

∞ ∞ ∞

Infinity's Choice

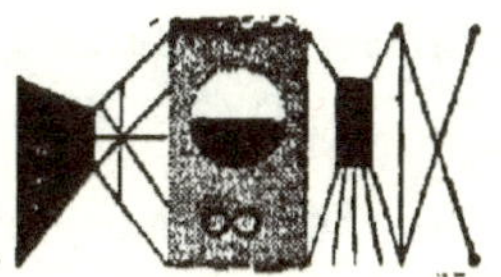

by DAMON KNIGHT

PEOPLE MINUS X, by Raymond Z. Gallun. Simon and Schuster, $3.00.

Raymond Z. Gallun's science fiction stories first began appearing in 1929. He is a skilled and resourceful writer, who unfortunately has what is probably the clumsiest touch with the English language since Austin Hall's. Groping at random, he pulls out a noun when he wants a verb, a verb when he wants a noun. His meaning shines dimly through a cloud of approximate words. His narrative sentences tumble out jerky and double-jointed. His dialogue is written exactly the same way, so that his characters can never converse normally, but always seem to be making speeches.

The far futures and alien intelligences of science fiction were Gallun's salvation in the thirties. If his characters spoke like nothing human, that only made them more plausible; and many of his stories of that period, such as "Old Faithful," "Davey Jones' Ambassador," and "Seeds of the Dusk," are among the most vivid and memorable stories about aliens ever written.

In the early forties, when science fiction was growing more realistic and somewhat less imaginative, Gallun dropped out of sight. He reappeared about 1950 and has kept turning up infrequently since, without attracting much notice. *People Minus X* is his first hard-cover book, and his first novel-length science fiction work of any kind.

The story begins with a young man, Ed Dukas, staring at a letter he has been writing, on which an invisible pen is tracing the word "Nipper." Ed's astonishment is documented at some length, but unconvincingly (he not only doesn't try to touch the hand which is presumably writing, but doesn't even have to repress the impulse to do so).

Then we get a flashback which lasts for 64 pages.

Ed's Uncle Mitch, the only man who ever called him "Nipper," disappeared after being partly responsible for a catastrophe in which the moon was destroyed, and 200,000,000 people killed.

Among the dead: Ed's father and a hen-pecked neighbor named Ronald Peyton. Neither had taken the then-common precaution of having his "body record" made. If they had, Humpty Dumpty could have been put together again: spanking new copies could have been manufactured, identical to the old down to the last cell. As it was, copies were made anyhow, based on memories of the victims' wives, friends and acquaintances.

These revenants were the "people minus X" of the title. They were almost, not quite, acceptable copies. Something was missing; a decade or so ago, it would have been called the soul. Sometimes the changes were trivial, sometimes comic: Peyton's overbearing wife remembered him as a brute, so the copy she got *was* a brute.

Some of the copies were physiologically human; others, however, were put together out of a new substance called vitaplasm, and they were stronger, tougher and more adaptable than normal people. As the years passed, racial antagonism against "the Phonies" increased; rabble-rousers appeared, there were outbreaks of violence, and somebody began manufacturing vitaplasm monsters to stir up still more prejudice.

Having remembered all this, Ed is arrested by police who have been spying on him with electronic eavesdropping devices, and who think he can lead them to Uncle Mitch. While Ed is in his cell, another message mysteriously appears on a scrap of paper he holds in his hand: " 'Nipper—argue police—you go Port Smitty—Mars—at once.' " Ed accordingly goes, marrying his girl and taking her along, and the police go too, keeping their distance like children playing hare and hounds.

Now Uncle Mitch, as you might have guessed, has used micro-miniaturization techniques (an idea that fascinated Gallun as long ago as 1936) to create an invisibly small duplicate of himself. It's this duplicate who wrote the messages, and who, riding along with Ed, directs him to the concealed laboratory in the Martian desert where his original body lies in suspended animation.

And here, 100 pages into the book, Gallun's story suddenly comes to life.

Ed and his wife Barbara consent to use the apparatus Uncle Mitch has left waiting, to make miniature duplicates of themselves. They lose consciousness in the tanks of the apparatus: they awaken in a microscopic wonderland.

"Close by, everything was slightly blurred, as if (they) were far-sighted. Farther off, objects became hazed, as by countless drifting, speeding dots that weren't opaque but that seemed—

each of them—to be surrounded by refractive rings that distorted the view of what lay beyond them."

Now, this is science fiction. It performs sf's specific function, to lift us out of here-and-now and show us marvels. No matter how badly it's written, if a story does that it is science fiction. A story that fails to do that, no matter how well written, isn't.

This story does it, eventually, with the vividness for whose sake sf readers have always been willing to swallow a little absurdity. (People in stories who blithely walk into matter transmitters, to be "broken down into their constituent atoms, and reassembled at the receiver," never seem to reflect that even though to the reassembled person, experience may seem to be continuous, to the original person, experience stops —in effect, it's death. In a similar way, Ed and Barbara seem blind to the fact that in consenting to have tiny copies made of themselves, they are dooming the copies to live out their lives in the world of smallness. The only route of return is via another copying, which is no return at all. As for vitaplasm, the stuff that enables the micro-people to live and function even in vacuum (Gallun says it is "capable of drawing its energy from sunlight or radioactivity"), this is nonsense or magic, certainly not science. But like Wells' "Cavorite" and a host of other improbable devices, it gets us to a place that common sense can't reach.)

Dust motes, to Ed and his friends, are jagged crystalline stones, or twisted masses like the roots of trees. When the police find the hidden laboratory and force their way in, the event has a titanic grandeur: "It seemed then that the mountains opened, unfolded, grew taller, disgorged Atlases. . . ." And: "The face, briefly glimpsed, was a huge, pitted mask, bearded with a forest of dark and tangled trunks."

Often enough, after this point, the story dips back into Gallun's muddled, pedestrian interpretations of the here-and-now. But in occasional passages, such as the heroes' epic, self-propelled journey from Mars to Earth, it touches the pure nerve of wonder. In places, even Gallun's leaden prose turns to poetry; for instance, listen to this: "spoke without sound in the stinging silence."

The full meaning of the story appears only after the ostensible plot is all done. The human-android conflict has been solved by leaving Earth to the humans—the androids can thrive anywhere. Spreading out, colonizing the planets of other stars, they are just beginning to realize the vastness of the experience ahead of them. Suns may turn cold and nebulas dim; the androids who are living now will still be there—changed, and yet the same—still on the move, still questing.

Gallun, who wrote this story once before, too ("Avalanche," by "Dow Elstar," in *Astounding,* December, 1935), sums up his vision in these words, near the end of the book:

"Inconceivably far off were other galaxies. Maybe Ed read her mind a little, as she thought of the vast, tilted swirl of the one in Andromeda. . . . As a child she used to look at a picture of it and think that everything she could imagine, and much more, was there: books, musical instruments, summer nights, dark horror."

∞

EARTHMAN'S RETURN, by Poul Anderson and Gordon R. Dickson. Gnome, $3.00.

Here are the five published Hoka stories, plus one new one, assembled into a more or less coherent narrative. The Hokas, for the benefit of any greenhorns in the audience, are chubby ursine inhabitants of a planet called Toka. They look like large teddy bears and have a constitutional weakness for play-acting, which they take with maniacal seriousness. In the first story, "The Sheriff of Canyon Gulch," Ensign Alexander Braithwaite Jones of the Terrestrial Interstellar Survey Service lands on Toka to find that the Hokas have swallowed a previous expedition's old Western movies chaps, spurs and sombrero. They herd reptilian "cattle," congregate in false-fronted saloons, and faithfully obey all human rites and customs—e.g., the dumbest man in town is always elected sheriff, while the official Town Gambler runs things.

In spite of some overcute writing, and a strong sense that only an abysmal idiot would ever let a Hoka read a book or magazine, see a movie or watch television *twice,* I find these things pretty funny. The plots are nothing much; the stories stand or fall on the Hokas as the medium for burlesque of (a) Westerns, (b) *Don Giovanni,* (c) space opera, (d) Sherlock Holmes, (e) the Spanish Main, and (f) the Foreign Legion. Except for the one new story, "Don Jones," which seems to me tasteless and labored, the narrative is a continuously lively stream, full of unexpected Hoka improvements on the human standard (e.g., " 'Belay that!' shouted the captain. 'Avast drowning . . .' "). My favorite, I guess, is "In Hoka Signo Vinces," the space-opera spoof, in which this immortal line occurs: " 'But if turning on the fire extinguisher sprinklers, the fumigation system, the leak-detector smoke system, the emergency radionic-heating system, the emergency refrigeration system, and directing the sewers into the deck-flushing system isn't a dirty way to fight, I'd like to know what is.' "

The five full-page Cartier illustrations are each and every one delightful. The stories originally appeared in *Other Worlds*, *Universe*, and *Fantasy and Science Fiction*.

∞ ∞ ∞

"So—20th Century women were broad-minded, eh?"

NOTE FOR A TIME CAPSULE

By EDWARD WELLEN

INFINITY

Yes, I know, the rating services probably never call you up. But they call me up twenty times a week!

Illustrated by RICHARD KLUGA

I TAKE IT you sociologists living in what to me is the future (I take it there's a future, a future with a place for sociologists) will note the unlikely revolution in taste now going on. For your information, then, here's why the rating services are reflecting a sudden upping from the pelvis to the cortex—just in case this will have become a cause for wild surmise.

You probably know what the rating services are ("were," to you; but I don't want to tense this document up). Most people nowadays don't know about the rating services; they know *of* them.

Every so often I hear someone say darkly, "I don't know about those polls. I've never had a call from them and no one I know has ever had a call from them."

I keep quiet or mumble something noncommittal. I could say, truthfully, "I *do* know about those polls. They ring me up more than twenty times a week." I could say that but I don't.

Not so much because I don't want to seem a crackpot or a liar as because I don't want to spoil a good thing. Or at least what I think is a good thing—and for the time being what I think is a good thing is what the world thinks is a good thing.

Now, in order for you to get the picture you must understand that the New York metropolitan area fashions the literary and musical fads of the United States and the United States by example and by infiltration via writings and movies and recordings fashions the fads of the world. And the New York metropolitan area goes by the opinions I frame.

It probably seems strange to you that I, in any amassing of statistics merely one digit in the neighborhood of the decimal point, can claim to exert such far-reaching influence.

But I've seen much the same sort of thing in my work as a CPA. Someone possessing relatively few shares in a holding company may exercise an inordinate amount of power over the national economy.

An analogous set of operations makes it possible for me to be an esthetic shot of digitalis in the body politic. That's why Barton's *Mikrokosmos* is at this writing the top tune and why archaeology professor Dr. Loob is high man on the polls with his TV show *Dig This!* and why the world has taken such a turn that you may very likely be calling this the Day of the Egghead.

But you're most likely asking at this point, "Why, in the name of statistical probability, did this character get so many calls when so many people got none?" And your next thought is, "Or did he? Was he a paranoiac?"

Here's my answer to your second question. I'm certainly not imagining any of this. You're bound to come upon some signs of these times and know what I've said about the revolution in taste is true. Otherwise there'd be no point in my setting this down or in your reading it.

The hard part is to convince you that the rest of it—about my role—is true. The trouble is there's nothing about me personally that would help me convince you. There's nothing uncommon about me except that my tastes were previously uncommon.

As I mentioned, I'm a CPA. I live in a suburb of New York City. I have an office in the city. I'm really semi-retired and take care of only a few old business friends, so my listing in the Manhattan phone directory doesn't include the terms CPA or ofc. I have a commutation book and the usual gripes against the NYNH&H. As a matter of fact I'm writing this while commuting and you'll have to blame not me but the roadbed and the rolling stock for any of this you may find difficult to decipher, for really I have a very neat handwriting. Although there's no noticeable pressure of work I stay on at my office after the girl's quitting time. (She still chews gum, but all day yesterday she was humming Bartok's *Mikrokosmos.*) I balance books until the line at the bottom of the column becomes a bongo board on a decimal point and then I squeeze my eyes and shake my head and go home.

I live alone. I'm a widower. I have one daughter. Thank goodness she's grown, married, and living in a place of her own, so there's no one to tie up the phone. I've given up frequenting the haunts of my old cronies. Though I miss their argumentative companionship I take comfort in the fact that I'm furthering our common interests. I don't give a hang that my lawn needs mowing; let the wind violin through the grass—I'm staying near the phone.

It's between six and seven in the evening at the office and between eight and midnight at home that I receive the calls.

That brings me to your first question—about why I consistently get so many calls when so many people get none.

Let me make it clear at once that even if the polls were buyable or fixable, and I'm not suggesting they are, I haven't the means to buy or the electronic knowledge to fix supposedly random calls. Besides, I'm fairly ethical.

Then what's the answer?

Naturally I've given this phenomenon more than a bit of thought, and I've formulated a theory to explain—at least to *my* satisfaction—why what's happening's happening. I believe the drawing power of my phone numbers inheres in the nature of number.

Now don't go getting hot under the collar—if you're still wearing collars—before you hear me out.

I'm not talking about numerology or any such mystical hocus-pocus. I'm talking about the psychopathology of everyday life. That's what's skewing and skewering the law of probabilities.

I know this demands explaining, so I'll be specific.

Apart from these calls from the rating services, I keep receiving calls on my home phone from people who set out to dial a certain undertaker—I beg his pardon, funeral director. We have the same exchange, in fact his number differs from mine only in that the first of his last four digits is a zero while my corresponding one is a nine.

Of course by now you've put your finger on it. These people are dialing the under— funeral director because, in the current colloquialism, someone's number's up. They misdial because they're unconsciously saying *nein* to the zero of death.

I've analyzed both my home phone number and my office phone number in this fashion, figuring out what their components connote singly and as gestalts. And I can see why these fortuitous combinings command attention, why these numbers leap out of the directory pages right at you. Privately I call such a number a common denominator with a way of accreting its numerator.

I hope you're not laughing at me.

AFTER ALL, when you remember what number is, what's happening follows naturally. Number's a language we use to blaze our way through the wood of reality. Without number we couldn't say what is more or less probable, we couldn't signpost our path. But using number is like trying to detect the emission of a photon without having to receive that photon. The difficulty lies in trying to get number at least one remove from the font of all language—the human mind. Possibly we'll come closest to order, be at one with reality, when we can order number—at the level of statistical probability—to be truly random, at one with chaos.

At any rate, there you have it. I'd like to go into greater detail but I'm afraid to.

Before my phone numbers up and atted 'em I was content merely to tune out the noisome and the fulsome and sigh to myself, "That's life. You ask for beer and get water."

That is, I thought I was content.

It's only now that I'm getting beer with an egg in it that I realize how passionately I hated the way things were and how passionately I'd hate to have to go back to that way.

I don't know how long this phenomenon will go on but while it lasts I mean to make the most of it.

I unashamedly enjoy watching the expression of bewildered enthusiasm on everyone's face. That expression is there because everyone listens to and looks at what the polls tell him is popular and because everyone tells himself he likes it because "everyone" likes it.

But in some respects my feelings are more uncertain. I'm glad and at the same time sorry for the longhair musicians. It seems more embarrassing than pleasing to them to find themselves suddenly the idols of bobby-soxers. I try not to think of Stravinsky barricading himself against the adulating adolescents souveniring him to his underwear.

As you can see, I've had to harden my heart. (It's tempting to say I've had to become number.) And I intend to be even more ruthless.

I'm planning, for example, to place on the Hit Parade Dhaly's *Concerto in Alpha Wave for Oscillograph and Woodwinds.*

That's why I'm being exceedingly careful to leave nothing to chance. Though this document is sort of a hostage to fortune, I'm taking into account the possibility that I might lose it while commuting and that it might fall into the hands of some unsympathetic contemporary. So I'm not writing down my phone numbers or my name. I want to keep the lines clear for the pollsters.

∞ ∞ ∞

Fanfare

SATELLITE IN THE SKY

By ANDY YOUNG

SO HERE WE ARE in the age of space travel. Although it is almost a month old by now, I still find it a rather unsettling thought that we will never again have a sky without man-made objects in it. By the time you read this, the Russians should have a second satellite up there; less than a month later the U. S. may have one up; and by the time the first one comes down there will be several others up there keeping each other company. By the time the last of the IGY satellites comes down, there will probably be a permanent robot satellite in orbit. The exploration of space will be a permanent part of our lives from now on.

The early weeks of the space era were marked chiefly by confusion. It was quite some time before the scientists themselves were able to decide what Sputnik was up to; there were mistaken reports that the satellite was to come down in a matter of hours (from England) while other reports were predicting lifetimes of several months (from Russia). Everyone was able to get into the act, and the opinions of scientifically ignorant generals and politicians (as well as those of a noisy planetarium director) were foisted upon the public with as much fervor as the wisest statements of the best-informed scientists. In comparing taped newscasts from various countries, it became clear to me that American reporters and newscasters were abysmally ignorant of the principles of celestial mechanics, both in comparison with the foreign reporters and on an absolute basis. It was pathetic to see these people telling the world that the satellite's period was increasing, so therefore it had slowed down and was about to crash; or, conversely, that the satellite was going faster and so should stay up longer than expected; or, worst of all, that it would probably stay up longer because the radio signals were gaining strength. How anybody could have gotten the idea that the radio transmitter was keeping the satellite up, I'll never know . . . I hope.

Of course, the newsmen had no monopoly on ignorance. Unfortunately enough, a politician is generally as much a scientific layman as the people he represents, and the people who make the most important decisions were generally as baffled on the subject of satellites as the general public. As a result, most of them didn't quite know what to make of the little oversize golf ball hanging over their heads.

Then there was the matter of the satellite "race": was it or wasn't it? Well, various officials have made it abundantly clear that there wasn't any race, officially. But it is also abundantly clear that everybody else considered it a race; you don't talk in worried tones about losing a race that doesn't exist. To say that there was no race *officially* is correct, but perhaps misleading; to deny that the race existed after you've lost is rather poor sportsmanship, and there were plenty of people who said flatly that we never were in a race. I don't think that anyone has ever said that the arms race is official, but everybody acknowledges its reality. Just as you don't have to declare a war to have a war, you don't have to officially announce a race in order to have a race.

Now the question arises: if there was a race, why didn't we try harder to win? There are, I think, two main answers to this. First of all, a lot of people in this country lived under the happy delusion that we would just naturally win. After all, we were first with the A-bomb and first with the H-bomb (and besides, it's obvious that we have to do everything first, because the Russians have to wait until their spies can steal the secret from us before they can copy us). Many people believed that Russian scientists were incapable of doing anything for themselves because of their lack of personal freedom. But there are many kinds of freedom; the personal variety has very little to do with the activities of a scientist doing research. The sort of freedom that is important for scientific work is the freedom to follow up any interesting lead, rather than mechanically doing a certain task. In this country there is a good deal of personal freedom, but scientists doing applied research do sometimes run into a shortage of scientific freedom; the Russians have a lack of political freedom, but apparently they have quite a bit of scientific freedom.

But there were a lot of people who knew what the Russian scientists could do, and indeed our intelligence service knew quite a while in advance that the Russians would put up a satellite this fall. Quite a number of people who could have speeded up our Project Vanguard knew that we would be beaten but did nothing. Why? Apparently, they thought that it would not make any difference. Possibly they pictured the Russian satellite as similar to our own: a small, lightweight, "impractical" scientific toy. I don't think many people were expecting the Russian satellite to be so big and heavy. But apparently many of these official types who sat around and did nothing did so because they thought the launching of a satellite would not produce the sensation it did.

Oddly enough, they were half right. For although the policymakers and the newscasters and the newspaper editors have worked up a cold sweat over the Sputnik, the public at large has been pretty blase about it. Editorials have cautioned us to avoid panic and hysteria; they are talking to themselves. How many people do you know who even went out to look for Sputnik? Only a handful out of every hundred. Foreign governments criticized the U. S. sharply for allowing the Russians to pull such a coup, but what was the reaction of the man in the street? The BBC interviewed a few people about London; a typical response was "They got there first, and jolly good luck to them." A woman interviewed said of Sputnik, "I think it's simply *ghastly,*" but her reason was that "we can't manage things properly here on Earth, so why should we go barging out into space?" rather than any concern over the East-West power struggle. In this country, a Boston paper asked a number of citizens what they thought of Sputnik. "The answers were amazing," the paper said, "Most of those interviewed conceded that launching of the satellite was significant, but they were too busy or lacked knowledge to be interested.

"Like this reaction of a taxicab driver: 'Gee, bud, I've been too busy all day to give it any thought.'

"Many persons were too engrossed in the World Series, the Little Rock situation and other issues to give much thought to the satellite.

"Even the vociferous park-bench 'experts' along the mall in Boston Common devoted serious discussion to other subjects."

Here are some of the things people said:

One woman said the disclosure of the satellite had a "scary" effect on her. "It makes you wonder what the Russians are up to—especially when you can't even see the thing up there." . . . "I have been reading about this plan for a year or so, but I thought the United States would have one first."

. . . "Now it's up to the United States to come up with a better satellite." . . . "It's a heck of a thing to let the Russians get ahead of us in a matter like this, but I guess we'll have a better one pretty soon." . . . "They sure have the technical ability in Russia. There's no doubt about that. But we should be optimistic about it. We'll have a better satellite."

And so on. Once when we went out to look for Sputnik and failed to see it, a fat man guiding two children home afterwards told us that *he* thought it wasn't a Russian satellite at all, but just a natural one that everybody was getting excited over for nothing. Another character, on another trip, said, "Yeah, but what good is it? It'll be a hundred years before you can do anything with it."

You notice that there is a widespread belief that *our* satellite will (of course) be *better*. President Eisenhower has said that ours will bring back more scientific information than theirs. This is hogwash, and wishful thinking. If they can put up a satellite five to ten times heavier than anything we will put up, they can, by the most elementary reasoning, put up in one satellite what we can put up in all six of ours; furthermore, the more generous load requirement will allow them to perform experiments we can't touch. It may be that we are somewhat better at miniaturizing our equipment, but I don't think we are capable of compressing equipment six times as far as the Russians can. There is every reason to expect that the Russians will get more results from their satellites than we will from ours. (An additional factor to consider is that the shell of our satellite is about half its weight, so that only about 10 pounds of equipment can be carried in each of ours, while the Russians must be able to devote about 150 pounds of their 184-pound bird to the instrumentation. Thus we would have to be ahead of them in miniaturization by a factor of 15 instead of 6 in order to do as well as they can on a satellite-for-satellite basis.) Furthermore, since our rocket vehicle is to work with a much smaller margin of error than the Russian rocket, we stand a pretty good chance of botching several tries. All this fine talk about having the better satellite will look pretty sick if our first two or three tries to put it up fail.

Now, what about the military and political consequences of Sputnik? It is a simple fact that the Russians are ahead of us in the development of the ICBM. This is another of those simple, self-evident truths that people in Washington have been trying to talk out of existence. It should be perfectly evident that if the Russians can make a rocket which will lift a heavy object like Sputnik to a height of 560 miles or so and put it in an orbit with an eccentricity of 5% or so, they can use the same rocket to shoot a bomb a shorter distance with more accuracy. The only step which they may not have solved is the re-entry problem: how to get the bomb back to the surface of the Earth intact, without burning it up. The President surely knows this; yet he has said that Sputnik did not worry him "one iota." It is true that little Sputnik *itself* is harmless; yet Eisenhower's statement would lead the uncritical to believe that the *fact* that the Russians were able to put it up is devoid of harmful implications.

We are going to learn the hard way that science is too important to be left to the politicians. And science in the U. S. today is being chiefly controlled by political non-scientists. Most of the research being done today is paid for by the Federal Government, and too little of this is "basic" research. A scientist working on an "applied" project might discover something that would suggest an important principle, but would be denied funds to look into it since the Government policy was not in favor of encouraging such basic-research offshoots of "practical" problems. It might also be added that the preparation of time-consuming, pointless, and unread reports for bureaucratic purposes is a further limitation on scientific freedom.

Here is the problem: We are at present fighting an economic and political war with Russian Communism. The possibility exists that some day we may be fighting a shooting war. Both the shooting war and the economic war, and possibly even the political war, can be decided by the rate at which the two sides make appropriate scientific discoveries. As an immediate example, consider the economic war. Suppose Russia were to discover a means of controlling hydrogen fusion before we do. This would give the Russians an almost unlimited supply of cheap power, since hydrogen is a lot cheaper and more common than uranium, and hydrogen fusion liberates a lot more energy than does uranium fission. Not only would the Russians have this power available for their own use, they would be able to offer it to other countries—India, for example. It is well known that the Russians would prefer to spread their influence over the world by such economic means rather than by force. If Russia were to get sufficiently ahead of the U. S. in such scientific accomplishments, it might quite possibly be able to take over the world by purely economic means.

∞

"Satellite in the Sky" has been condensed from a special fanzine of the same name, published by Andy Young for the Fantasy Amateur Press Association.

And Then Took Off

Live in Superior, Ohio, and see the world—but watch out for nervous submarines!

the Town

A Book-length Novel

By RICHARD WILSON

Illustrated by ED EMSH

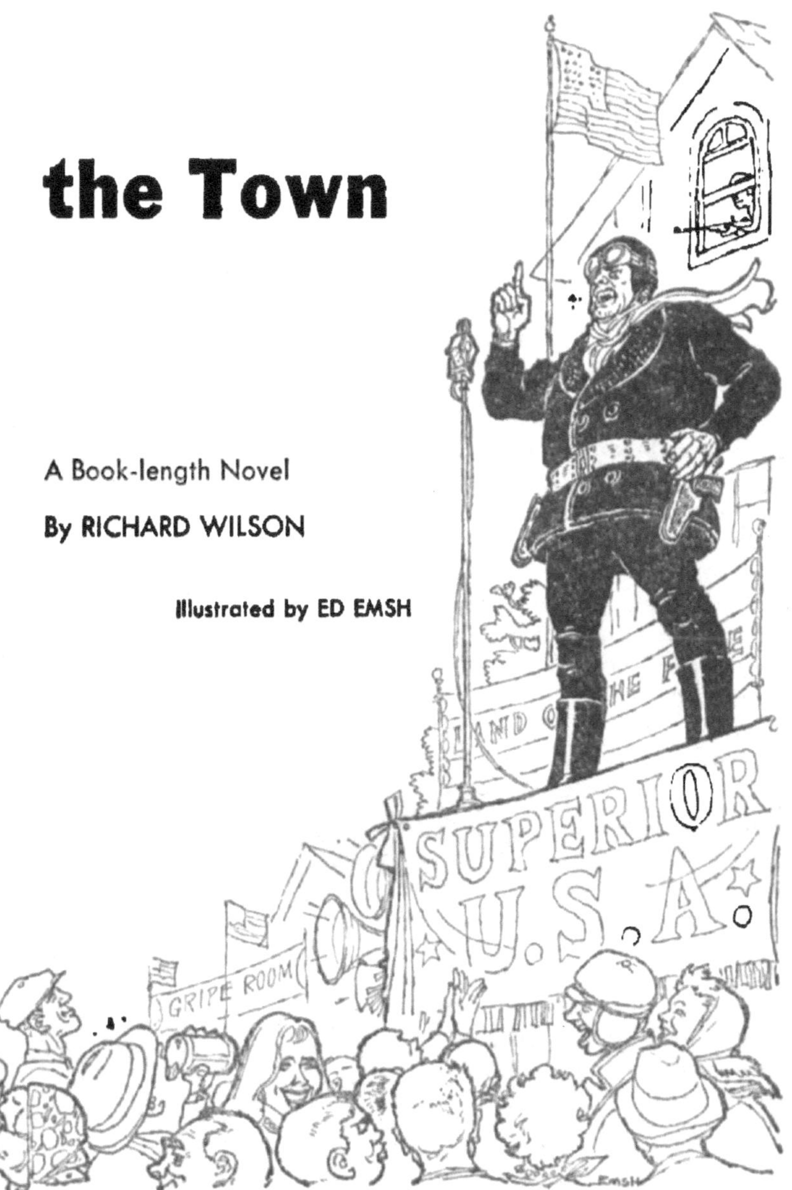

And Then the Town Took Off

By Richard Wilson

Synopsis of Part One:

SUPERIOR, Ohio, took off at midnight on October 31. It flew straight up, taking with it a good chunk of the surrounding real estate and a train that had been passing through. The passengers from the train, like the population of the town, had no way of getting down off Superior or getting Superior itself back to Earth.

Among the passengers were Don Cort, an Army sergeant masquerading as a bank messenger and carrying an important brief case to Washington; and Geneva Jervis, secretary to the flamboyant Senator "Bobby the Bold" Thebold. Don's disguise became even more complicated when he discovered the brief case contained a fanatically compact radio transceiver; the Pentagon ordered him to wear this under his clothing so that they could test it and listen in on events in Superior at the same time. The events in question were enough to make him dizzy.

Osbert Garet, Professor of Magnology at Superior's Cavalier Institute, appeared to be trying to take the credit for lifting the town without actually saying so. Mayor Hector Civek issued a proclamation saying Superior had seceded from the Earth. Newspaper editor Ed Clark and leading citizen Doc Bendy figured something should be done, but they didn't know quite what. Alis Garet, the professor's pretty and level-headed daughter, helped Don do some investigating, but the results were inconclusive.

"Bobby the Bold" and his cohorts in Private Pilots buzzed the town in their war-surplus P-38's, but the only result was that one plane crashed and the pilot had to parachute back to Earth. Jen Jervis and Don searched a mysterious tunnel and found a room full of strange equipment, and reports of strange creatures began trickling in.

Then Mayor Civek proclaimed himself King—and was immediately kidnapped by two odd kangaroo-like animals.

Now Read Part Two:

CHAPTER XVI

HECTOR CIVEK hadn't been found by the time Judge Helms' court convened at 10 a.m.

Joe Negus was there, wearing a new suit and looking confident. His confederate, Hank Stacy, was obviously trying to achieve the same poise but not succeeding. Jerry Lynch, their lawyer, was talking to Ed Clark.

Don Cort took a seat the editor had saved for him in the front row. Alis Garet came in and sat next to him. "I cut my sociology class," she told him. "Anybody find His Majesty yet?"

"No," Don said. "Who gave him that crackpot idea?"

"He's had big ideas ever since he ran for the state assembly. He got licked then but this is the first time he's been kidnaped. Or should it be kanganaped? Poor Hector. I shouldn't joke about it."

Judge Helms, who was really a justice of the peace, came in through a side door and the clerk banged his gavel. But the business of the court did not get under way immediately. Someone burst in from the street and shouted:

"He's back! Civek's back!"

The people at the rear of the room rushed out to see. In a moment they were crowding back in behind Hector Civek's grand entrance.

"Oh, no," Alis said. "Don't tell me he made it this time!"

Civek was wearing the trappings of royalty. He walked with dignity down the aisle, an ermine robe on his shoulders, a crown on his head and a sceptre in his right hand.

He nodded benignly about him. "Good morning, Judge," he said. To the clerk he said, "Frank, see to our horses, will you?"

"Horses?" the clerk said, blinking.

"Our royal coach is without, and the horses need attending to," Civek said patiently. "You don't think a king walks, do you?"

The clerk went out, puzzled. Judge Helms took off his pince-nez and regarded the spectacle of Hector Civek in ermine.

"What is all this, Hector?" he asked. "You weren't serious about that king business, were you? Nice to see you back safe, by the way."

"We would prefer to be addressed the first time as Your Majesty, Judge," Civek said. "After that you can call us sir."

"Us?" the judge asked. "Somebody with you?"

"The royal 'we,' " Civek said. I'll have to issue a proclamation on the proper forms of address. I mean, *we*'ll have to. Takes a bit of getting used to, doesn't it?"

"Quite a bit," the judge agreed. "But right now, if you don't mind, this court is in session and has a case before it. Suppose you make your royal self comfortable and we'll get on with it—as soon as my clerk is back from attending to the royal horses."

The clerk returned and whispered in the judge's ear. Helms looked at Civek and shook his head. "Six of them, eh? I'll have a look later. Right now we've got a bank robbery case on the calendar."

Vincent Grande talked and Jerry Lynch talked and Judge Helms listened and looked up statutes and pursed his lips thoughtfully. Joe Negus cleaned his nails. Hank Stacy bit his.

Finally the judge said: "I hate to admit this, but I'm afraid I must agree with you, counselor. The alleged crime contravened no local statute and in the absence of a representative of the federal government I must regretfully dismiss the charges."

Joe Negus promptly got up and began to walk out.

"Just a minute there, varlet!"

It was Hector Civek doing his king bit.

Negus, who probably had been called everything else in his life, paused and looked over his shoulder.

"Approach!" Civek thundered.

"Nuts, your kingship," Negus said. "Nobody stops me now." But before he got to the door something stopped him in mid-stride.

Civek had pointed his sceptre at Negus in that instant. Negus, stiff as a stop-action photograph, toppled to the floor.

"Now," Civek said, motioning to Judge Helms to vacate the bench, "we'll dispense some royal justice."

He sat down, arranging his robes and shifting his heavy crown. "Mr. Counselor Lynch, we take it you represent the defendants?"

"Yes, Your Majesty," said the lawyer, an adaptable man. "What happened to Negus, sir? Is he dead?"

"He could have been, if we'd given him another notch. No, he's just suspended. Let him be an example to anyone else who might incur our royal wrath. Now, counselor, we are familiar enough with the case to render an impartial verdict. We find the defendants guilty of bank robbery."

"But Your Majesty," Lynch said, "bank robbery is not a crime under the laws of Superior. I submit that there has been no crime—inasmuch as the incident occurred after Superior became detached from Earth, and therefore from its laws."

"There is the King's Law," Civek said. "We decree bank robbery a crime, together with all other offenses against the county, state and country which are not specifically covered in Superior's statutes."

"Retroactively?" Lynch asked.

"Of course. We will now pronounce sentence. First, restitution of the money, except for ten per cent to the King's Bench. Second, indefinite paralysis for Negus. We'll straighten out his arms and legs so he'll take up less room. Third, probation for Hank Stacy here, with a warning to him to stay out of bad company. Court's adjourned."

CIVEK wouldn't say where he'd got the costume or the coach-and-six or the paralyzing sceptre. He refused to say where the two kangaroo-like creatures had taken him. He allowed his ermine to be fingered, holding the sceptre out of reach, talked vaguely about better times to come now that Superior was a monarchy, then ordered his coach.

By royal decree Hank Stacy, who had been inching toward the door, became royal coachman, commanded to serve out his probation in the king's custody. Stacy drove Civek home. No one seemed to remember who had been at the reins when the coach first appeared.

CHAPTER XVII

ED CLARK was setting type for an extra when Don and Alis visited his shop.

KING'S IN BUSINESS, the headline said.

"You don't sound like a loyal subject," Don said.

"Can't say I am," Clark admitted. "Guess I won't get to be royal printer."

"What's the story about?" Alis asked. "The splendid triumph of justice in court this morning?"

"No. Everybody knows all about that already. I've got the inside story—what happens next. Just like *The New York Times.*"

"Where'd you get it?" Don asked.

Clark winked. "Like Scotty Reston, I am not at liberty to divulge my sources. Let's just say it was learned authoritatively."

"Well," Alis said, "what does happen next?"

"Listen," the editor said, and he read:

"His Unconstitutional Majesty, King Hector I, will attempt to prop up his shaky monarchy by seeking an ambassador from the United States, the *Sentry* learned today.

"Such recognition, if obtained, would be followed immediately by a demand for 'foreign aid.'

"It is the thesis of the self-proclaimed king—known until 24 hours ago as just plain Hector—that the satellite status of Superior, the traveling townoid, makes it a potentially effective object of U. S. diplomacy.

"King Hector will point out to the State Department the benefits of bolstering Superior's economy, especially during its expected foray over Europe and, barring such misfortune as being shot down en route, into the Soviet domain.

"The King will not suggest in so many words that Superior would make a good spy platform, but the implication is there. It will also be implied that unless economic aid—which in plain English means food and fuel to keep Superior from starving and freezing to death—is forthcoming from the United States, Superior may choose the path of neutrality. . . ."

"That's as far as I've got," Clark said.

"I suppose 'the path of neutrality' means Superior might consider hiring itself out to the highest bidder?" Don asked.

"That would be one way to put it," Clark said. "Undiplomatic but accurate."

"How does Civek intend to get his message to Washington?" asked Don, aware that it had already been transmitted to the Pentagon via the transceiver under his collar. "Bottle over the side?"

"My sources tell me they've got WCAV working on short wave. That right, Alis?"

"Don't ask me. I only live there."

"Do you still think Civek is fronting for the Cavalier crowd?" Don asked her.

"I don't remember saying that," she said. "I think I agreed with you when you said Civek was ineffectual. Who do *you* think is behind him? Do you think he's king of the kangaroos?"

"Well," Don said, "they're the ones who took him away last night. And when he came back this morning he had all the trappings. He didn't get that coach-and-six from foreign aid."

Ed Clark said: "This is all very fascinating, kids, but it's not helping me get out my extra. Don, why don't you take the little lady out to lunch? You can continue your theorizing over the blue plate special at the Riverside Inn. Only place in town still open, they tell me."

Doc Bendy was hurrying out of the Riverside Inn as they reached it. He waved to them. "Save your money. His Gracious Majesty is throwing a free lunch for everybody."

"Where?"

"At the palace, of course."

"What palace?" Alis asked.

"The bubble gum factory. He's taken it over."

"Why the gum factory?"

"Cheeky McFerson offered it to him. Not the factory itself but the big old house near the west wing. The mansion that's been closed up since the old man died. They say Cheeky's been given a title as part of the bargain."

"Sir Cheeky?" Alis asked, giggling.

"Something like that. Lord Chicle, maybe, or Baron de

Mouthful. Come on. It should be quite a show."

Dozens of people were in the streets, all heading in the same direction. Word of the king's largesse spread fast and, on the factory grounds, guards were directing the crowd to a line that disappeared into a side door of the old McFerson mansion.

A flag flew from the top of a pole at the front of the house. It was whipping in a stiff breeze and Don couldn't make out the device, except that a crown formed part of it.

One of the guards recognized Alis Garet and directed her to the front door. She took Doc Bendy and Don by their arms. "Come on," she said. "We're VIPs. Father must have sworn allegiance."

The chief of police was sitting behind a desk in the wide front hall but he now wore a military tunic with a chestful of decorations (including the Good Conduct Ribbon, Sergeant Cort noticed), and the visor of his military cap was overrun with gold curlicues.

"Well, Vince," Bendy said. "I see you got in on the ground floor."

"General Sir Vincent Grande, Minister of Defense," Grande said with a stiff little bow, "at your service."

"Enchanted," Bendy said, bowing back. "Tell me, Vince, how do you keep a straight face?"

"I'll overlook that, Bendy, and I'll give you a friendly tip. The country is on a sound basis now and we intend to keep it that way. Obstructionists will be dealt with."

"The country, eh? Well, let's go in and see how it's being run."

A clattery hubbub came from the big room on the right. To Don it sounded like any GI mess hall. It also looked like one. The line of people coming in through the side door helped themselves to tin trays and silverware, then moved slowly past a row of huge pots from which white-coated men and women ladled out food. At the end of the serving line stood Cheeky McFerson, splendid in purple velvet. He was putting a piece of bubble gum on each tray.

On the other side of the room, opposite the servers, King Hector sat on a raised chair, crown on head, sceptre in hand, nodding benevolently to anyone who looked at him. On each side of the king, sitting in lower chairs, were members of what must have been his court. Professor Osbert Garet was one of them and Maynard Rubach, president of the Cavalier Institute of Applied Sciences, was another.

"Oh, dear, there's father," Alis said in dismay. "What is that silly hat he's wearing? It makes him look like Merlin."

"But Civek doesn't look a bit like King Arthur," Bendy said. "Let's go pay our respects. Straight faces, now."

"Ah, my dear," the king said when he saw Alis. "And gentlemen. Welcome to our court. May we introduce two of our associates? Sir Osbert Garet, Royal Astronaut, and Lord Rubach, Minister of Education."

"Father!" Alis spoke sharply to the Royal Astronaut. "How silly can you get?"

"Now, now, child," the king said reprovingly. "You must not risk our displeasure. For the time being our rule must be absolute—until the safety of our kingdom has been assured. Sir Osbert," he said, "we trust that at a more propitious time you will have a serious talk with your charming but impetuous daughter."

"My liege, I shall deal with her," the Royal Astronaut said, glowering at Alis. "As Your Majesty has so wisely observed, she is but a slip of a girl."

Her father's apparent sincerity left Alis speechless. She looked from Bendy to Don, but they seemed to consider discretion and masklike faces the better part of candor.

"Well spoken, Sir Osbert," the king said. He clapped his hands and a servant jumped up. "Dinner for these three. Find a table, my friends, and you will be served."

Don firmly guided Alis away. She had seemed about to explode. They found an empty table out of earshot of the king, and three footmen looking like refugees from Alice in Wonderland immediately began to serve them.

Bendy spread a napkin over his lap. "Let's curb our snickers and fill our stomachs," he said, "and later we can go out behind the barn and laugh our heads off. Meanwhile keep your eyes open."

THEY WERE EATING meat loaf and potatoes. The meat loaf was so highly spiced that it could have been almost anything.

"I wonder where his worship got all the grub," Alis said.

"I don't know," Don said, "but it certainly doesn't look as if he needs any foreign aid."

Alis put down her fork suddenly and her eyes got big. She said, "You don't suppose—"

"Suppose what?" Bendy said, spearing a small potato.

"I just had a horrible thought." She laughed feebly. "It's ridiculous, of course, but I wondered if by any chance we were eating Joe Negus."

"Don't be silly," Don said, but he put down his fork too.

"Of course it's ridiculous," Bendy said. "Hector only put Negus to sleep. He didn't kill him. Besides, Joe Negus wouldn't stretch far enough to feed this crowd."

"Is that why you're not eating any more?" Alis asked him.

"Why, no," Bendy said. "It's merely that I've had enough. It's true that Hector could have used his sceptre on other transgressors, but— No, I refuse to admit that he's turned cannibal."

"*He* isn't eating," Don pointed out.

"I'll guarantee you he has, though. I've never known Hector to miss a meal. No. Hector may be a fool and a dupe, and power-hungry to boot, but he's not a cruel man, or a deranged one."

"No?" Alis said. "I dare you to ask him what's in the meat loaf."

"All right." Bendy got up. "I'll ask to see the kitchen—to compliment the chef. Want to come?"

"No, thanks. I might be mean to father again."

She and Don watched Doc Bendy go to the improvised throne and talk to Civek. The king laughed and stood up and he and Bendy crossed the room. They went through a door behind the line of servers.

Don pushed his plate away. "You've certainly spoiled my appetite."

"I'm sorry," Alis said. "Maybe it's hereditary. Look at father in that idiot hat. Sir Osbert! Honestly, Don, if we ever get back to Earth I'm going to get out of Superior as fast as I can. What's it like in Washington?"

"Dull," he said. "Humid in the summer. And when you've exhausted the national monuments there's nothing to do."

"Nothing? Don't tell me you don't have a girl friend back there. No, *don't* tell me—I don't want to know. Oh, Don, what a terribly boring place this must be for you."

"Boring!" he said. "I've never had such a wild, crazy time in my life. Furthermore," he said, "there's nobody like you back in Washington."

She beamed. "I'd kiss you right here, only Doc Bendy's coming back. Heck, I'll kiss you anyway."

She did.

"Ahem," said Bendy. "Also cough-cough. If you two can spare the time, there's someone I'd like you to meet."

"We're through, for now," Alis said. "Who?"

"One of our hosts. The power behind the shaky throne of Hector the First. I think you'll like him. He has a magnificent tail."

CHAPTER XVIII

"HECTOR was very cooperative," Doc Bendy said. "I guess he figured he couldn't keep it a secret for long anyhow, so he decided to be frank. After all, half the town had seen them take him away."

"You mean Civek admits he's

only a figurehead?" Don asked.

"Oh, he wouldn't admit that. His story is that it's a working arrangement—a treaty of sorts. He's absolute monarch as far as the human inhabitants are concerned, but the kangaroos control Superior as a piece of geography."

"I knew father couldn't have done it," Alis murmured.

They went down a flight of stairs off the main hall to a basement room. It was luxuriously furnished, as every room in the mansion must have been. There was a rug over inlaid linoleum and a fireplace blazing. A huge round mahogany table stood in the center of the room.

Hector Civek sat in one of the half dozen leather armchairs drawn up to the table. In another sat a furry, genial-looking blue-gray kangaroo.

Only it wasn't really a kangaroo, Don realized. It was more human than animal in several ways. Its bearing, for instance, had dignity and its round eyes had intelligence. A thick tail at least three feet long stuck through a space under the backrest of the armchair. As Doc Bendy had said, the tail was magnificent.

Civek nodded and smiled, apparently willing to forget his flare-up at Alis. "I'll introduce you," Civek said. "I mean *we'll* introduce you— Oh, the hell with the royal we, as long I'm among friends. This is Gizl, and what I'm trying to say is that he doesn't speak English. Doesn't talk at all, as far as I can tell. But he understands the language and he can read and write it. That's why all this."

He indicated the letter and number squares on the table. They were from sets of games—Scrabble, Anagrams, I-Qubes, Lotto and poker dice.

"My granddaughter met Gizl, you'll recall," Doc Bendy said. "Either this one or one like him. We don't know yet whether Gizl is a personal name or a generic one."

"Let's find out," Don said. He sat down at the table and began to form squares into words asking a question.

"Wait a minute." Doc Bendy broke up Don's sequence. "The amenities first. Spell out 'Greetings,' or some such thing. Manners, boy."

"Sorry." Don started over. He spelled GREETINGS, then ALIS GARET, then DON CORT, and pointed from the squares to Alis and himself. "I assume you've already introduced yourself?" he asked Bendy.

Bendy nodded and the kangaroo-like creature inclined his furry head in acknowledgment to Alis and Don. Then he—Don had already stopped thinking of the creature as an "it"—formed two words with his tapering, black-nailed fingers.

PLEASANT, he communicated. GIZL. And he tapped his chest three times.

Don turned to Bendy. "Now can I ask him?"

"With His Majesty's permission," Bendy said solemnly.

Hector nodded. Don left the three names intact, distributing the rest, then put three squares together to spell MAN. He pointed to it and then to Civek, Bendy, Alis and himself, excluding the creature.

"Well, I like that!" Alis said. "Do I look like a man?"

"Let's keep it simple, woman," Don said.

The creature nodded and pointed again to GIZL, then to himself. "He doesn't understand," Don said.

"It's quite possible his people don't have individual names," Bendy said. "Let's call him Gizl for now and go on."

"Okay." Don thought for a moment, then formed a question. "Might as well get basic," he said.

Q. ARE YOU FROM EARTH
A. NO

At the risk of irritating the others, Don repeated the questions and answers aloud for the benefit of his eavesdropper in the Pentagon.

Q. ARE YOU FROM SOLAR SYSTEM
A. NOT YOURS
Q. WHEN DID YOU REACH EARTH
A. 1948 YOUR CALENDAR
Q. WHY
A. FRIENDSHIP
Q. WHY HAS NO ONE SEEN YOU SOONER
A. FEAR
Q. YOU MEAN YOU FRIGHTENED OUR PEOPLE
A. NO I MEAN FEAR OF YOUR PEOPLE
Q. WHY
A. GIZL RESEMBLE EARTH ANIMALS
Q. WAS SUPERIOR THE FIRST PLACE YOU LANDED
A. NO
Q. WHERE WAS IT
A. AUSTRALIA

"The home of the kangaroo," Doc Bendy said. "No wonder they had a bad time. I can imagine some stockman in the outback taking umbrage at a kangaroo asserting its equality. Let me talk to him a while, Don."

Q. HOW MANY ARE THERE OF YOU
A. MANY
Q. HOW MANY
A. NO SPECIFIC COMMENT
Q. ARE YOU RESPONSIBLE FOR RAISING SUPERIOR
A. ENTIRELY
Q. HOW
A. IMPOSSIBLE TO EXPLAIN WITH THESE

Q. Where is Superior going

A. East for now

Q. And later

A. No specific comment

Q. 3000 lives are in your hands

A. Gizls have no malevolent designs

Q. Thanks. You said friendship brought you. What else

A. Trade. Cultural exchange

Q. WHAT HAVE YOU TO TRADE

A. WILL DISCUSS THIS LATER WITH DULY CONSTITUTED AUTHORITY

Q. WHO KING HECTOR

A. TERMINATING INTERVIEW WITH GOODWILL ASSURANCES

"Wait," Alis said. "I haven't had a chance to talk to him." She formed letters into words. "I don't think he's being very frank with

us but I have a few random questions."

Q. How many sexes have Gizls
A. Three
Q. Male female and
A. Neuter
Q. Are there babies among you
A. Babies are neuter and develop according to need
Q. Confidentially what do you think of father's science
A. Unfathomable our meager knowledge
Q. Flatterer
A. Ending conversation with pleasant regard
Q. Likewise

Gizl slid back his chair and got up. King Hector stood and bowed as Gizl, who had nodded politely to each in turn, walked, manlike without hopping, to a corner of the room which then sank out of sight.

"He's quite a guy, that Gizl," Hector said, taking off his crown and putting it on the table. "Makes me sweat," he said, wiping his forehead.

"Are you the duly constituted authority?" Bendy asked him.

"Who else? Somebody's got to be in charge till we get Superior back to Earth."

"Sure," Bendy said, "but you don't have to rig yourself up in ermine. I also have a sneaking suspicion that you aren't exactly anxious to get Superior down in a hurry."

"I'll overlook that remark for old time's sake. But I defend the kingship. A show of force was necessary to prevent crime from running rampant."

"Maybe," Bendy said. "Anyhow I appreciate your frankness in introducing us to Gizl and what he modestly describes as his meager knowledge. Since you've already admitted that he's the one who provided the big feed, will you ease Alis's mind now and assure her that what she was eating wasn't Negusburger?"

"Negusburger?" The king laughed. "Is that what you thought, Alis?"

"Not really," she said. "But I couldn't help wondering where all the food came from all of a sudden."

"Over here." The king led them to the corner where Gizl had sunk from sight. The top of the elevator, now level with the floor, blended exactly with the linoleum tile. In a moment it rose again. "I don't know how it works, but Gizl and his people have their headquarters down there somewhere. All I have to do is write an order and send it down. Up comes food or whatever I need. Would you like to try it?"

"Love to," Bendy said. "What shall I ask for?"

"Anything."

"*Any*thing?"

"Anything at all."

"Well." Bendy looked impressed. "This will take a moment of thought. How about a gallon—no; as long as I'm asking I might as well ask for a keg—of rum, 151 proof."

Up it came, complete with spigot and tankard.

"Fabulous!" Bendy said. He rolled it out of the elevator and the elevator went down again as soon as it was empty.

"Let me try!" Alis said. "If Doc can get a keg, I ought to be able to have—oh, say a pint of Chanel Number 5. Would that be too extravagant?"

"A simple variation in formula, I should think," the king said. He wrote out her request.

What came up for Alis didn't look in the least like an expensive Paris perfume. In fact, it looked like a lard pail with a quantity of liquid sloshing lazily in it. But its aroma belied its completely unappetizing looks.

"Oh, heaven!" Alis said. "Smell it!" She lifted it by its handle, stuck a finger in it and rubbed behind each ear.

"It's a bit overpowering by the pint," Bendy said. He'd drained off a tankard of rum and looked quite at peace with the world. "You'd better get yourself a chaperone, Alis, if you're going to carry that around with you."

"I'll admit they're not very good in the packaging department but that's just a quibble. Could I have—how many ounces in a pint?—sixteen one-ounce stoppered bottles? And a little funnel?"

"Easiest thing in the world," the king said. "Don? Anything you'd like at the same time? Save it a trip."

"I've got an idea, Your Majesty, but I don't know whether you'd approve. Even though I work in a bank, I've never seen a ten thousand dollar bill. Do you think they could whip one up?"

"I really don't know," Hector said. "It could upset the economy if we let the money get out of hand. But we can always send it right back. Let's see what happens."

The elevator came up with the bottles, the funnel and a green and gold bill.

It was, on the face of it, a ten thousand dollar bill. But the portrait was that of Hector Civek, crowned and ermined. And the legend on it was:

Payable to Bearer on Demand, Ten Thousand Dollars. This Note is Legal Tender for all Debts, Public and Private, and is Redeemable in Lawful Money at the Treasury of the Kingdom of Superior. (Signed) Gizl, Secretary of the Treasury.

CHAPTER XIX

Don didn't know what he might learn by skulking around the freezing grounds of Hector's palace in the faint moonlight. He hoped for a glimpse of the kangaroo-Gizl to see if he were as sincere off-guard as he had been during their interview.

But his peering into basement windows had revealed nothing and he was about to head back to the campus for a night's sleep when someone called his name.

It was a girl's voice, from above. He looked up. Red-headed Geneva Jervis was leaning out of one of the second-story windows.

"Well, hello," he said. "What are you doing up there?"

"I've sworn fealty," she said. "Come on up."

"What?" he said. "How?"

She disappeared from his sight, then reappeared. "Here." She dropped a rope ladder.

Don climbed it, feeling like Romeo. "Where'd you get this?"

"They've got them in all the rooms. Fire escape. Old McFerson was a precautious man, evidently." She pulled the rope back in.

Jen Jervis had a spacious bedroom. She wore a dressing gown.

"What do you mean you swore fealty?" Don asked. "To Hector?"

"Sure. What better way to find out what he's up to? Besides, I was getting fed up with that dormitory at Cavalier. No privacy. House mothers creeping around all the time. Want a drink?"

Don saw that she had a half-full glass on the dresser next to a bottle of bourbon with quite a bit gone from it.

"Why not?" he said. "Let's drink and be merry, for tomorrow we may freeze to death."

"Or be shot down by Reds." She poured him a stiff one. "Here's to happy endings."

He sipped his drink and she swallowed half of hers.

"I didn't picture you as the drinking type, Jen."

"Revise the picture. Come sit down." She backed to the big double bed and relaxed into it, lying on one elbow.

Don sat next to her, but upright. "Tell me about this fealty deal. What did you have to do?"

"Oh, renounce my American citizenship and swear to protect Superior against all enemies, foreign and domestic. The usual thing."

"Have you got a title yet? Are you Dame Jervis?"

"Not yet." She smiled. "I think I'm on probation. They know I'm close to Bobby and they'd like to have him on their side, for all their avowed independence. They're not so terribly convinced that Superior's going to stay up forever. They're hedging their bets, it looks to me."

"It looks to me that maybe Bobby Thebold might not understand. He's the kind of man who demands absolute fealty, from what I've seen of him."

"Oh, to hell with Bobby Thebold." Jen took another swallow. "He's not here. He's had plenty of time to come, if he was going to, and he hasn't. To hell with him. Let me get you another drink."

"No, thanks. This will do me fine." He drank it and set the empty glass on the floor. Jen drank off the last of hers and put her glass next to his.

"Relax," she said. "I'm not going to bite you." She lay back and her dressing gown opened in a V as far as the belt. She obviously wasn't wearing anything under the gown.

Don looked away self-consciously.

Jen laughed. "What's the matter, boy? No red blood?" She rolled herself off the end of the bed and went to the dresser. "Another drink?"

"Don't you think you've had enough?"

She shook her red hair violently. "Drinking is as drinking does. Trouble is, nobody's doing anything."

"Exactly. Everybody's acting as if Superior's one big pleasure dome. Civek's on the throne and all's well with his little world. Even you've joined the parade. Why? I don't buy that double agent explanation."

She was looking in the bureau mirror at the reflection of the top of her head, peering up from under her eyebrows. "I'm going to have to touch up the tresses pretty soon or I won't be a redhead any more." She looked at his reflection. "You don't like me, do you, Donny-boy?"

"I never said that."

"You don't have to say it. But I don't blame you. I don't like myself sometimes. I'm a cold fish. A cold, dedicated fish. Or I was. I've decided to change my ways."

"I can see that."

"Can you?" She turned around and leaned against the bureau, holding her glass. "How do you see me now?"

"As an attractive woman with a glass in her hand. I wonder which is doing the talking."

"Rhetorical questions at this time of night, Donny? I think it's me talking, not the whiskey. We'll know better in the sober light of morning, won't we?"

"If that's an invitation," Don began, "I'm afraid—"

Her eyes blazed at him. "I think you're the rudest man I ever met. *And* the most boorish." She tossed off the rest of her drink, then began to cry.

"Now, Jen—" He went to her and patted her shoulder awkwardly.

"Oh, Don." She put her head

against his chest and wept. His arms automatically went around her, comfortingly.

Then he realized that Jen's muffled sobs were going direct to the Pentagon through his transceiver. That piece of electronics equipment taped to his skin, he told himself, was the least of the reasons why he could not have accepted Jen's invitation—if it had been an invitation.

He lifted her chin from his chest to spare the man in the Pentagon any further sobs, which must have been reaching him in crescendo. Jen's face was tear-stained. She looked into his eyes for a second, then fastened her mouth firmly on his.

There was nothing a gentleman could do, Don thought, except return the kiss. Rude, was he?

Jen broke away first. "What's that?" she said.

Don opened his eyes and his glance went automatically to the door. It would not have surprised him to see King Hector coming through it in his royal night clothes. But Jen was staring out the window. He turned.

The sky was bright as day over in the direction of the golf course. Don made out a pinpoint of brighter light.

"It's a star shell," he said. "A flare."

They went to the window and leaned out, looking past a corner of the bubble gum factory.

"What's it for?" Jen asked.

Don pointed. "There. That's what for."

"A blimp!" she said. "It's landing!"

"Is it an Air Force job? I can't make out the markings."

"I think I can," Jen said. "They're—P.P."

"Private Pilots! Senator Bobby the Bold!"

Jen Jervis clutched his arm. "S.O.B.!" she whispered fiercely.

CHAPTER XX

DON CORT was down the rope fire escape and away from the mansion before it woke up to the invasion. As he crossed the railroad spur he had a glimpse of Jen Jervis hauling up the rope and of lights going on elsewhere in the building. There was a lot of whistle blowing and shouting and a lone shot which didn't seem to be aimed at him.

Don waited at the spur, behind a boxcar, to see how the Hectorites would react to the landing of the blimp. A few men gathered at the front gate and looked nervously into the sky and toward the golf course. Others joined them, armed with shotguns, pistols and a rifle or two, but not with King Hector's paralysis gadget.

It was clear that Hector had no intention of starting a battle. His men apparently were under orders only to guard the mansion and the bubble gum factory. No one even went to see what the blimp was up to.

Don found as he neared the golf course that the people from the blimp apparently had no immediate plan to attack, either. He found a sand trap to lie down in. From it he could watch without being seen. The star shell had died out but he could see the blimp silhouetted against the sky. Men in battle dress were establishing a perimeter around the clubhouse. Each carried a weapon of some kind. It was all very dim.

Don remembered his communicator. "Cort here," he said softly. "Do you read me?"

"Affirmative," a voice said. Don didn't recognize it. He described the landing and asked: "Is this an authorized landing or is it Senator Thebold's private party?"

"Negative," said the voice from the Pentagon, irritatingly GI.

"Negative *what?*" Don said. "You mean Thebold *is* leading it?"

"Affirmative," said the voice.

"What's he up to?" Don asked.

"Negative," the voice said.

Don blew up. "If you mean you don't know, why the hell don't you say so? Who is this, anyhow?"

"This happens to be Major Johns, the O.O.D., Sergeant, and if you know what's good for you . . ."

Don stopped listening because a man in battle dress, apparently attracted by his voice, was standing on the green, looking down into the bunker where Don lay, pointing a carbine at him.

"I'll have to hang up now, Major," Don said quietly. "Something negative has just happened to me. I've been captured."

The man with the carbine shouted down to Don: "Okay, come out with the hands over the head."

Don did so. He hoped he was doing it affirmatively enough. He had no wish to be shot by one of the Senator's men, regardless of whether that man was authorized or unauthorized.

SENATOR THEBOLD sat at a desk in the manager's office of the Raleigh Country Club. He wore a leather trench coat and a fur hat. Wing commander's insignia glittered on his shoulders and a cartridge belt was buckled around his waist. A holster hung from it but Thebold had the heavy .45 on the desk in front of him. He motioned to Don to sit down. Two guards stood at the door. They looked alert and tough.

"Name?" Thebold snapped.

Don decided to use his own name but pretend to be a local yokel.

"Donald Cort."

"What were you doing out there?"

"I saw the lights."

"Who were you talking to in the sand trap?"

"Nobody. I sometimes talk to myself."

"Oh, you do? Do you ever talk to yourself about a man named Osbert Garet or Hector Civek?" Thebold looked at a big map of Superior that had been pinned to the wall, thus giving Don the benefit of his strong profile.

"Hector's the king now," Don said. "Things got pretty bad before that but we got enough to eat now."

"Where did the food come from?"

Don shrugged.

Thebold drummed his fingers on the desk. "You're not exactly a fount of information, are you? What do you do for a living?"

"I used to work in the gum factory but I got laid off."

"Do you know Geneva Jervis?"

"Who's he?" Don said innocently.

Thebold stood up in irritation. "Take this man to O. & I.," he said to one of the guards. "We've got to make a start someplace. Are there any others?"

"Four or five," the guard said.

"Send me the brightest looking one. Give this one and the rest a meal and a lecture and turn them loose. It doesn't look as if Civek is going to give us any trouble right away, and there isn't too much we can do before daylight in any event."

The guard led Don out of the room and pinned a button on his lapel. It said: *Bobby the Bold in Peace and War.*

"What's O. & I.?" Don asked him.

"Orientation and Integration. Nobody's going to hurt you. We're here to end partition, that's all."

"End partition?"

"Like in Ireland. Keep Superior in the U.S.A. They'll tell you all about it at O. & I. Then you tell your friends. Want some more buttons?"

DON WAS FED, lectured and released, as promised.

Early the next morning, after a cup of coffee with Alis Garet at Cavalier's cafeteria, he started back for the golf course. Alis, in a class-cutting mood, went with him.

The glimpses of the Thebold Plan which Don had had from O. & I. were being put into practice. Reilly Street, which provided a boundary line between Raleigh Country Club and the gum factory property, had been transformed into a midway.

The Thebold forces had strung bunting and set up booths along the south side of the street. Hector's men, apparently relieved to find that the battle was to be psychological rather than physical, rushed to prepare rival attractions on their side.

A growing crowd thronged the center of Reilly Street. Some wore Thebold buttons. Some wore other buttons, twice as big, with a smiling picture of Hector I on them. Some wore both.

The sun was bright but the air was bitingly cold. As a result one of the most popular booths was on Hector's side of the street where Cheeky McFerson was giving away an apparently inexhaustible supply of hand warmers. Cheeky urged everybody to take two, one for each pocket, and threw in generous handfuls of bubble gum.

Two of Hector's men set up ladders and strung a banner across two store-fronts. It said in foot-high letters: KINGDOM OF SUPERIOR, LAND OF PLENTY.

A group of Thebold troubleshooters watched, then rushed away and reappeared with brushes and paint. They transformed an advertising sign to read, in letters two feet high: SUPERIOR, U.S.A., HOME OF THE FREE.

Hawkers on opposite sides of the midway vied to give away hot dogs, boiled ears of corn, steaming coffee, hot chocolate, candy bars and popcorn.

"There's a smart one." Alis pointed to a sign in Thebold territory. THE GRIPE ROOM, it said over a vacant store. The Senator's men had set up desks and chairs inside and long lines had already formed.

Apparently a powerful complaint had been among the first to be registered because a Thebold man was galvanized into action. He ran out of the store and within minutes the sign painters were at work again. Their new banner, hoisted to dry in the sun, proclaimed: BLIMP MAIL.

Underneath, in smaller letters, it said: *How long since you've heard from your Loved Ones on Earth? The Thebold Blimp will carry your letters and small packages. Direct daily connections with U. S. Mail.*

"You have to admire them," Alis said. "They're really organized."

"One's as bad as the other," Don said. Impartially, he was eating a Hector hot dog and drinking Thebold coffee. "Have you noticed the guns in the upstairs windows?"

"No. You mean on the Senator's side?"

"Both sides. Don't stare."

"I see them now. Do you see any Gizl-sticks? The thing Hector used on Negus?"

"No. Just conventional old rifles and shotguns. Let's hope nobody starts anything."

"Look," Alis said, grabbing Don by the arm, "isn't that Ed Clark going into the Gripe Room?"

"It sure is. Gathering material

for another powerful editorial, I guess."

But within minutes Clark's visit had provoked another bustle of activity. Two of Thebold's men dashed out of the renovated store and off toward the country club. They came back with the Senator himself, making his first public appearance.

Thebold strode down the center of the midway, wearing his soft aviator's helmet with the goggles pushed up on his forehead and his silk scarf fluttering behind him. A group of small boys followed him, imitating his self-confident walk and scrambling occasionally for the Thebold buttons he threw to them. The Senator went directly into the Gripe Room.

"Looks as if Ed has wrangled an interview with the great man himself," Alis said.

"You didn't say anything to Clark about our talk with the Gizl, did you?"

"I did mention it to him," Alis said. "Was that bad?"

"Half an hour ago I would have said no. Now I'm not so sure."

A SPEAKER'S PLATFORM had been erected on the Senator's side of Reilly Street, and now canned but stirring band music was blaring out of a loudspeaker. Thebold came out of the Gripe Room and mounted the platform. A fair-sized crowd was waiting to hear him.

Thebold raised his arms as if he were stilling a tumult. The music died away and Thebold spoke.

"My good friends and fellow Americans," the Senator began.

Then a Hectorite sound apparatus started to blare directly across the street. The sound of hammering added to the disruption as workmen began to set up a rival speaker's platform. Then the music on the north side of Reilly Street became a triumphal march and Hector I made his entrance.

Thebold spoke on doggedly. Don heard an occasional phrase through the din. ". . . reunion with the U.S.A. . . . end this un-American, this literal partition . . ."

But many in the crowd had turned to watch Hector, who was magnificent and warm-looking in his ermine robe.

"Loyal subjects of Superior, I exhort you not to listen to this outsider who has come to meddle in our affairs," Hector said. "What can he offer that your king has not provided? You have security, inexhaustible food supplies and, above all, independence. . . ."

Thebold increased his volume and boomed:

"Ah, but *do* you have independence, my friends? Ask your puppet king who provides this food—and for what price? And how secure *do* you feel as you whip through the atmosphere like an unguided missile? You're over the Atlantic now. Who knows at what second the unearthly controls may break down and dump us all into the freezing waters. . . ."

Hector pushed his crown back on his head as if it were a derby hat. "Who asked the Senator here? Let me remind you that he does not even represent our former—and I emphasize *former*—State of Ohio. We all know him as a political adventurer, but never before has he attempted to meddle in the affairs of another country. . . ."

". . . and you know what lies beyond Western Europe," Thebold said. "Eastern Europe and Russia. Atheistic, communistic Red Russia. Is that where you'd like to come down? For that's where you're heading under Hector Civek's so-called leadership. King Hector, he calls himself. Let me remind you, friends, that if there is anything the Red Soviet Russians hate more than a democracy, it's a monarchy—and I don't like to think what your chances would be if you came down in Kremlinland. Remember what they did to the Czars."

Then Senator Bobby Thebold played his ace:

"But there's an even worse possibility, my poor misguided friends. And that's for the creatures behind Hector Civek to decide to go back home—and take off into outer space. Has Hector told you about the creatures? He has not. Has he told you they're aliens from another planet? He has not. Some of you have seen them—these kangaroo-like creatures who, for their own nefarious purposes, made Hector what he is today.

"But, my friends, these are not the cute and harmless kangaroos that abound in the land of our friendly ally, Australia. No; these are intelligent alien beings who have no use for us at all and who have brazenly stolen a piece of American territory and are now in the process of making off with it."

A murmur came from the crowd and they looked over their shoulders at Hector, whose oratory had run down and who seemed unsure how to answer.

"Yes, my friends," Thebold went on, "you may well wonder what your fate will be in the hands of that power-mad ex-mayor of yours. A few thousand feet more of altitude and Superior will run out of air. Then you'll really be free of the good old U.S.A. because you'll be dead of suffocation. That, my friends—"

AT THAT POINT somebody took a shot at Senator Bobby Thebold. It missed him, breaking a second-story window behind him.

Immediately a Thebold man behind that window smashed the rest of the glass and fired back across Reilly Street, over the heads of the crowd.

People screamed and ran. Don grabbed Alis and pulled her away from the immediate zone of fire. They looked back from behind a truck which until a minute ago had been dispensing hot buttered popcorn.

"Hostilities seem to have commenced," Alis said. She gave a nervous laugh. "I guess it's my fault for blabbing everything to Ed Clark."

"It was bound to happen, sooner or later," Don said. "I hope nobody gets hurt."

Evidently neither Thebold nor Hector personally had any such intention. Both had clambered down from the platforms and disappeared. Most of the crowd had fled, too, heading east toward the center of town, but a few, like Alis and Don, had merely taken cover and were waiting to see what would happen next.

Sporadic firing continued. Then there was a concentration of shooting from the Senator's side and a dozen or more of Thebold's men made a quick rush across the street and into the stores and buildings on the north side. In a few minutes they returned, under another protective burst, with prisoners.

"Slick," Don said. "Hector's being out-maneuvered."

"I wonder why the Gizls aren't helping him."

The Thebold loudspeaker came to life. "Attention!" it boomed in the Senator's voice. "Anyone who puts down his arms will be given safe conduct to the free side of Reilly Street. Don't throw away your life for a dictator. Come over to the side of Americanism and common sense." There was a pause, and the voice added: "No reprisals."

The firing stopped.

The Thebold loudspeaker began to play *On the Sunny Side of the Street.*

But nobody crossed over. Nor was there any further firing from Hector's side.

Lay Down Your Arms, the loudspeaker blared in another topical tune from Tin Pan Alley.

When it became clear that Hector's forces had withdrawn completely from the Reilly Street salient, Thebold's men crossed in strength.

They worked their way block by block to the grounds of the bubble gum factory and proceeded to lay siege to it.

CHAPTER XXI

WITH HECTOR CIVEK immobilized, Senator Bobby Thebold went looking for Geneva Jervis, accompanied by two armed guards.

He was trailed by the usual pack

of small boys, several of them dressed in imitation of their hero in helmets, silklike scarves and toy guns at hips.

Alis, unable to reach the besieged palace to see if her father was safe, had asked Don to go back with her to Cavalier after the Battle of Reilly Street. Her mother told Alis that the Professor was not only safe on the campus but had resigned his post as Royal Astronaut at Hector's court.

"Father broke with Hector?" Alis asked. "Good for him! But why?"

"He and Dr. Rubach just up and walked out," Mrs. Garet said. "That's all I know. Your father never explains these things to me. But if my intuition means anything, the Professor is up to one of his tricks again. He's been locked up in his lab all day."

The campus had an air of expectancy about it. Students and instructors went from building to building, exchanging knowing looks or whispered conversations.

A rally was in progress in front of the administration building when Senator Thebold arrived. Don and Alis joined the group of listeners for camouflage and pretended to pay attention to what the speaker, an intense young man on the back of a pickup truck, was saying.

"The time has come," he said, "for men and women of, uh, perspicacity to shun the extremes and tread the middle path. To avoid excesses as represented on the one hand by the, uh, paternalistic dictatorship of the Hectorites and on the other by the, uh, pseudo-democracy of Senator Thebold which resorts to force when thwarted. I proclaim, therefore, the course of reason, the way of science and truth as exemplified by the, uh, the Garet-Rubach, uh—"

Senator Thebold had been listening at the edge of the little crowd. He spoke up.

"The Garet-Rubach Axis?" he suggested.

The speaker gave him a cold stare. "And who are you?"

"Senator Robert Thebold, representing pseudo-democracy, as you call it. Speak on, my young friend. Like Voltaire, I will defend to the death—but you know what Voltaire said."

"Yes, sir," the speaker said, abashed. "No offense intended, Senator."

"Of course you intended offense," Thebold said. "Stick to your guns, man. Free academic discussion must never be curtailed. But at the moment I'm more interested in meeting your Professor Garet. Where is he?"

"In—in the bell tower, sir. Right over there." He pointed. "But you can't go in. No one can." He looked at Alis as if for confirmation. She shook her head.

"We'll see about that," the Senator said. "Carry on with your free and open discussion. And remember, stick to your guns. Sorry I can't stay."

He headed for the bell tower, followed by his guards.

Alis waited till he had gone in, then tugged at Don's sleeve. "Come on. Let's see the fun."

"Alis," the speaker called to her, "was that really Senator Thebold?"

"Sure was. But what's this Garet-Rubach Axis? What's everybody up to?"

"Not Axis. That was Thebold's propaganda word. It's a movement of— Oh, never mind. You don't appreciate your own father."

"You can say that again. Come on, Don."

As Alis closed the door to the bell tower behind them, they heard Professor Garet's voice from above.

"Attention interlopers," it said. "You have come unasked and now you find yourself paralyzed, unable to move a muscle except to breathe."

"Stay down here," Alis whispered. "There's a sort of vestibule one flight up. That's where Thebold must have got it. Father spends all his spare time fortifying his holy of holies. Nobody gets past the vestibule." She frowned. "But I didn't know he had a paralysis thing, too."

"He probably swiped it from Hector before he broke with him," Don said.

Professor Garet's voice came again. "I shall now pass among you and relieve you of your weapons. Why, if it isn't Senator Thebold and his strong-arm crew! I'm honored, Senator. Here we are: three archaic .45s disposed of. Very soon now you'll have the pleasure of seeing a scientific weapon in action."

DON, standing with Alis on the steps of the administration building, didn't know whether to be impressed or amused by the giant machine Professor Garet had assembled. It was mounted on the flat bed of an old Reo truck and various parts of it went skyward in a dozen directions. Garet had driven it onto the campus from a big shed behind the bell tower.

The machine's crowning glory was a big bowl-shaped sort of thing that didn't quite succeed in looking like a radar scanner. It was at the end of a universal joint which permitted it to aim in any direction.

"What's it supposed to do?" Don asked.

"From what I gather," Alis said, "it's Hector's paralysis thing, adapted for distance. Only of course nobody admits father stole it. It's supposed to have anti-gravity powers, too, like whatever it was that took Superior up in the first place. Naturally I don't believe a word of it."

SUPERIOR

"But where's he going with it?"

"He's ready to take on all comers, I gather. Please don't try to make sense out of it. It's only father."

The young man who had addressed the student rally took over the driver's seat and Professor Garet hoisted himself into a bucket seat at the rear of the truck near a panel which presumably operated the machine. Maynard Rubach sat next to the driver. The small army of dedicated students who had been assembling fell in behind the truck. They were unarmed, except with faith.

Senator Thebold and his two former bodyguards, de-paralyzed, sat trussed up in the back of a weapons carrier, looking disgusted with everything.

"Are we ready?" Professor Garet called.

A cheer went up.

"Then on to the enemy—in the name of science!"

Don shook his head. "But even if this crazy machine could knock out Hector's and Thebold's men and the Garet-Rubach Axis reigns supreme, then what? Does he claim he can get Superior back to Earth?"

Alis said only, "Please, Don . . ."

The forces of science were ready to roll. There had been an embarrassing moment when the old Reo's engine died but a student worked a crank with a will and it roared back to life.

The Garet machine, the weapons carrier and the foot soldiers moved off the campus and onto Shaws Road toward Broadway and the turn-off for the country club.

They met an advance party of the Thebold forces just north of McEntee Street. There were about twenty of them, armed with carbines and submachine guns. As soon as they spotted the weird armada from Cavalier they dropped to the ground, weapons aimed.

Senator Thebold rose in his seat. "Hold your fire!" he shouted to his men. "We don't shoot women, children or crackpots." He said to Professor Garet: "All right, mastermind, untie me."

CHAPTER XXII

A SUBMARINE surfaced on the Atlantic, far below Superior.

It was obvious to the commander of the submarine, which bore the markings of the Soviet Union, that the runaway town of Superior, being populated entirely by capitalist madmen, was a menace to humanity. The submarine commander made a last-minute check with the radio room, then gave the order to launch the guided missiles which would rid the world of this menace.

The first missile sped skyward.

Superior immediately took evasive action.

First, in its terrific burst of acceleration, everybody was knocked flat.

Next, Superior sped upward for a few hundred feet and everybody was crushed to the ground.

At the same time the first missile, which was now where Superior would have been had it maintained its original course, exploded. A miniature mushroom cloud formed.

The submarine fired again and a second missile streaked up.

Superior dodged again. But this time its direction was down. Everyone who was outdoors—and a few who had been under thin roofs—found himself momentarily suspended in space.

Don and Alis, among the hundreds who had had the ground snatched out from under them, clung to each other and began to fall. All around them were the various adversaries who had been about to clash. Professor Garet had been separated from his machine and they were following separate downward orbits. Many of Thebold's men had dropped their guns but others clung to them, as if it were better to cling to something than merely to fall.

The downward swoop of Superior had taken it out of the immediate path of the second missile but whoever had changed the townoid's course had apparently failed to take the inhabitants' inertia into immediate consideration. The missile was headed into their midst.

Then two things happened. The missile exploded well away from the falling people. And scores of kangaroo-like Gizls appeared from everywhere and began to snatch people to safety.

Great jumps carried the Gizls into the air, and they collected three or four human beings at each leap. The leaps appeared to defy gravity, carrying the creatures hundreds of feet up. The Gizls also appeared to have the faculty of changing course while airborne, saving their charges from other loose objects, but this might have been illusion.

At any rate, Geneva Jervis, who had been hurled up from the roof of Hector's palace, where she had gone in hopes of catching a glimpse of Senator Thebold, was re-united with the Senator when they were rescued by the same Gizl, whose leap had carried him in a great arc virtually from one edge of Superior to the other.

Don Cort, pressed close to Alis and grasped securely against the hairy chest of their particular rescuer, was experiencing a combination of sensations. One, of course, was relief at being snatched from certain death.

Another was the delicious closeness of Alis, who he realized he hadn't been paying enough attention to in a personal way.

Another was surprise at the

number of Gizls who had appeared in the moment of crisis, just when they were needed.

Finally he saw beyond doubt that it was the Gizls who were running the entire show—that Hector I, Bobby the Bold and the pseudo-scientific Garet-Rubach Axis were merely strutters on the stage.

It was the Gizls who were maneuvering Superior as if it were a giant vehicle. It was the Gizls who were exploding the enemy missiles. And it was the alien Gizls who, unlike the would-be belligerents among the Earthpeople, were scrupulously saving human lives.

"Thanks," Don said to his rescuing Gizl as it set him and Alis down gently on the hard ground of the golf course.

"Don't mention it," the Gizl said, then leaped off to save others.

"He talked!" Alis said.

Don watched the Gizl make a mid-air grab and haul back a man who had looked as if he might otherwise have gone over the Edge. "He certainly did."

"Then that must have been a masquerade, that other time—all that mumbo-jumbo with the Anagrams."

"It must have been, unless they learn awfully fast."

He and Alis clutched each other again as Superior tilted. It remained steady otherwise and they were able to see the ocean, whose surface was marked with splashes as a variety of loose objects fell into it. Don had a glimpse of Professor Garet's machine plummeting down in the midst of most of Superior's vehicular population.

"There's a plane!" Alis cried. "It's going after something on the surface."

"It's the Hustler," Don said. "It's after the submarine."

The B-58's long pod detached itself, became a guided missile, and hit the submarine square in the middle. There was a whooshing explosion, the B-58 banked and disappeared from sight under Superior, and the submarine went down.

"SERGEANT CORT," a voice said, and because Alis was lying with her head on Don's chest she heard it first.

"Is that somebody talking to you, Don? Are you a sergeant?"

"I'm afraid so," he said. "I'll have to explain later. Sergeant Cort here," he said to the Pentagon.

"Things are getting out of hand, Sergeant," the voice of Captain Simmons said.

"Captain, that's the understatement of the week."

"Whatever it is, we can't allow the people of Superior to be endangered any longer."

"No, sir. Is there another submarine?"

"Not as far as we know. I'm talking about the state of anarchy in Superior itself, with each of three factions vying for power. Four, counting the kangaroos."

"They're not kangaroos, sir, they're Gizls."

"Whatever they are. You and I know they're creatures from some other world and I've managed to persuade the Chief of Staff that this is the case. He's in seeing the Defense Secretary right now. But the State Department isn't buying it."

"You mean they don't believe in the Gizls?"

"They don't believe they're interplanetary. Their whole orientation at State is toward international trouble. Anything interplanetary sends them into a complete flap. We can't even get them to discuss the exploration of the moon, and that's practically around the corner."

"What shall we do, sir?"

"Between you and me, Sergeant—" Captain Simmons' voice interrupted itself. "Never mind that now. Here comes the Defense Secretary."

"Foghorn Frank?" Don asked.

"Shh."

Frank Fogarty had earned his nickname in his younger years when he commanded a tugboat in New York harbor. That was before his quick rise in the shipbuilding industry where he got the reputation as a wartime expediter that led to his Cabinet appointment.

"Is this the gadget?" Don heard Fogarty say.

"Yes, sir."

"Okay. Sergeant Cort?" Fogarty boomed. "Can you hear me?" It was no wonder they called him Foghorn.

"Yes, sir," Don said, wincing.

"Fine. You've been doing a topnotch job. Don't think I don't know what's been going on. I've heard the tapes. Now, son, are you ready for a little action? We're going to stir them up at State."

"Yes, sir," Don said again.

"Good. Then stand up. No, better not if Superior is still gyrating. Just raise your right hand and I'll give you a field promotion to major. Temporary, of course. I can do that, can't I, General?"

Apparently the Chief of Staff was there, and agreed.

"Right," Fogarty said. "Now, Sergeant, repeat after me . . ."

Don, too overwhelmed to say anything else, repeated after him.

"Now then, Major Cort, we're going to present the State Department with what they would call a *fait accompli*. You are now Military Governor of Superior, son, with all the power of the U. S. Defense Establishment behind you. A C-97 troop carrier plane is loading. I'll give you the ETA as soon as I know it. A hundred paratroopers. Arrange to meet them at the golf course, near the blimp. And if Senator Thebold tries to interfere—well, handle him tactfully. But I think he'll go along. He's got his headlines and by now he should have been able to find his missing lady friend. Help him in that personal matter if you can. As for Hector Civek and Osbert Garet, be firm. I don't think they'll give you any trouble."

"But, sir," Don said. "Aren't you underestimating the Gizls? If they see paratroops landing they're liable to get unfriendly fast. May I make a suggestion?"

"Shoot, son."

"Well, sir, I think I'd better go try to have a talk with them and see if we can't work something out without a show of force. If you could hold off the troops till I ask for them . . ."

Foghorn Frank said: "Want to make a deal, eh? If you can do it, fine, but since State isn't willing to admit that there's such a thing as an intelligent kangaroo, alien or otherwise, any little deals you can make with them will have to be unofficial for the time being. All right—I'll hold off on the paratroopers. The important thing is to safeguard the civilian population and uphold the integrity of the United States. You have practically unlimited authority."

"Thank you, Mr. Secretary. I'll do my best."

"Good luck. I'll be listening."

"As I SEE IT," Alis said after Don had explained his connection with the Pentagon, "Senator Thebold licked Hector Civek. Father, who defected from Hector, captured the Senator and vice versa. But now the Gizls have taken over from everybody and you have to fight them—all by your lonesome."

"Not fight them," Don said. "Negotiate with them."

"But the Gizls are on Hector's side. It seems to come full circle. Where do you start?"

Superior had returned to even keel and Don helped her up. "Let's start by taking a walk over to the bubble gum factory. We'll try to see the Gizl-in-Chief."

There didn't seem to be anyone on the grounds of the McFerson place. The boxcar which had been on the siding near the factory was gone. It was probably at the bottom of the Atlantic by now, along with everything else that hadn't been fastened down. Don wondered if Superior's gyrations had been strong enough to dislodge the train that had originally brought him to town. The Pennsylvania Railroad wouldn't be happy about that.

They saw no one in the mansion and started for the basement room in which they'd had their talk with the Gizl, passing through rooms where the furniture had been knocked about as if by an angry giant. They were stopped en route by Vincent Grande, ex-police chief now Minister of Defense. "All right, kids," he said, "stick 'em up. Your Majesty," he called, "look what I got."

Hector Civek, crownless but still wearing his ermine, came up the stairs. "Put your gun away, Vince. Hello, Alis; hello, Don. Glad to see you survived the earthquake. I thought we were all headed for kingdom come."

Vincent protested: "This is that traitor Garet's daughter. We can hold her hostage to keep her father in line."

"Nuts," the king said. "I'm getting tired of all this foolishness. I'm sure Osbert Garet is just as shaken up as we are. And that crazy Senator, too. All I want now is for Superior to go back where it came from, as soon as possible. And that's up to Gizl, I'm afraid."

"Have you seen him since the excitement?" Don asked.

"No. He went down that elevator of his when the submarine surfaced. I guess his control room, or whatever it is that makes Superior go, is down there. Let's take a look. Vince, will you put that gun away? Go help them clean up the mess in the kitchen."

Vincent Grande grumbled and went away.

In the basement room, Hector went to the corner and said, "Hey! Anybody down there?"

A deep voice said, "Ascending," and the blue-gray kangaroo-like creature appeared. He stepped off the elevator section. "Greetings, friends."

"Well," Hector said, "I didn't know you could talk."

"Forgive my lack of frankness," Gizl said. "Alis," he said, bowing slightly. "Your Majesty."

"Frankly," Hector said, "I'm thinking of abdicating. I don't think I like being a figurehead. Not when everybody knows about it, anyhow."

"Major Cort," Gizl said.

Don looked startled. "What? How did you know?"

"We have excellent communications. We thank your military for its assistance with the submarine."

"A pleasure. And we thank you and your people for saving us when we went flying."

"Mutuality of effort," Gizl said. "I'll admit a dilemma ensued when the submarine attacked. But our obligation to safeguard human lives outweighed the other alternative—escape to the safety of space. Now suppose we have our conference. You, Major, represent Earth. I, Rezar, represent the survivors of Gorel-zed. Agreed?"

"Rezar?" Don said. "I thought your name was Gizl. And what's Gorel-zed?"

"Little Marie Bendy called me Gizl," Rezar said. "She couldn't pronounce Gorel-zed. I'm afraid I haven't been entirely candid with you about a number of things. But I think I know you better now. I heard your conversation with Foghorn Frank."

Don smiled. "Do you mean you've been listening in ever since I strapped on the transceiver?"

"Oh, yes," Rezar said. "So recapitulation is unnecessary. But we Gizls, so-called, are still a mystery to you, of course. I suppose you'd like some background. Where from, where to, when, and all that."

"I certainly would," Don said. "So would everybody else, I imagine, especially King Hector here and Mr. Fogarty."

"By all means let us communicate on the highest level," Rezar said. "First, where from, eh?"

"Right. Are you listening, Mr. Secretary?"

"I sure am," Fogarty said. "What's more, son, you're being piped directly into the White House—and a few other places."

"Good," Rezar said. "Now marvel at our saga."

CHAPTER XXIII

THE END of a civilization is a tragic thing.

On the desert planet of Gorel-zed, the last world to survive the slow nova of its sun, the Gizls, once the pests but now through brain surgery the possessors in their hardy bodies of the accumulated knowledge of the frail human beings, were preparing to flee. Their self-supporting ships were ready, capable of crossing space to the ends of the universe.

But their universe was barren. No planet could receive them. All were doomed as was theirs, Gorel-zed. They set out for a new galaxy, knowing they would not reach it but that the descendants might. They became nomads of space, self-sufficient.

For generations they wandered, their population diminishing. Their scientist-philosophers evolved the theory that accounted for their spaceborn ennui with life, their acceptance of their fate, their eventual doom. They had no roots, no place of their own. They had only the mechanistic world of their ships—which were vehicles, not a land. They must find a home of their own, or die.

Several times in their odyssey they had come to a planet which could have housed them. But each time an injunction which had been built into them at the time of the brain surgery prevented them from staying. The doomed human beings on Gorel-zed had built into the very fiber of the Gizls—who were, after all, only animals—the injunction that no human being could be harmed for their comfort.

This meant the world of Ladnora, whose gentle saffron inhabitants were incapable of offering resistance, could not be conquered. The Ladnorans, in their generosity, had offered the refugees from Gorel-zed a hemisphere of their own. But the Gizls required a world of their own, not a half-world. They accepted a small continent only and made it spaceborne and took it with them.

The Crevisians were the next to be visited. They ruled a belt of fertile land around the equator of their world—the rest was icy waste. The Gizls took a slice of each polar region and, joining them, made them spaceborne.

In time they reached the system of Sol.

Mars attracted them first because of its sands. Mars was like Gorel-zed in many ways. But that very resemblance meant it was not for them. Mars was a dead world, as their own Gorel-zed had become.

But next nearest Sol to Mars was a green planet. The Gizls moored the acquisitions in the asteroid belt and visited Earth.

Here, at their planetfall, Australia, was the perfect land. Even its inhabitants—the great kangaroos, the smaller wallabies—breathed Home to the Gizls. But there were also the human beings who had made the land their own. And though memory of their origin had weakened in the Gizls, the injunction had not.

For a time they set up a kind of camp in the great central desert and with delight found their legs again. Out of the cramped ships they came, to bound in freedom and fresh breathable air across the wasteland. But hardy naked black human beings lived in the desert, and they attacked the Gizls with their primitive weapons. And when the Gizls fled, not wishing to harm them, they came to white men, who attacked them with explosive weapons.

And so they took to their ships and were spaceborne again. But the attraction of Earth was strong and they sought another continent, called North America.

And in the center of it they found a great race whose technology was nearly as great as their own. These people had an intelligence and drive which rivaled that of their human antecedents, whose minds had been transferred to the Gizls' hardy, cumbersome bodies.

REZAR paused. His intelligent eyes seemed misplaced in his heavy animal body.

"What attracted you to Superior, of all places?" Alis asked.

Rezar seemed to smile. "Two things. Cavalier and bubble gum."

"What?" Alis said. "You're kidding!"

"No," Rezar said. "It's true. Bubble gum because after generations of subsistence on capsule food our teeth had weakened and loosened—and bubble gum strengthened them. Nourishment, no. Exercise, yes. And Cavalier Institute because here were men who spoke in terms which paralleled the secret of our space-drive."

Alis laughed. "This would make father expire of joy," she said. "But now you know he's just a phony."

"Alas," Rezar said. "Yes, alas. But he was so close. Magnology. Cosmolineation. It's jargon merely, as we learned in time. Osbert Garet is mad. Harmless, but mad."

CHAPTER XXIV

DON ASKED Rezar: "But if this built-in morality of yours is so strong, why didn't it prevent you from taking off with Superior?"

Rezar replied: "There are factions among us now. An evolution of a sort, I suppose. Nothing is static. One faction—" he tapped his chest "—is completely bound by the injunction. But in the other, self-preservation places a limit on the injunction."

The explanation seemed to be that the other faction, which grew in strength with every failure to find a world of their own, felt that a planet such as Earth, with a history of men warring against men, required the Gizls to be no more moral than the human inhabitants themselves.

"The Good Gizls versus the Bad Gizls?" Alis asked.

Rezar seemed to smile. The Bad Gizls, led by one called Kaliz, had got the upper hand for a time and elevated Superior, intending to join it to the bits and pieces of other planets they had previously collected and stored in the asteroid belt. But Rezar's influence had persuaded them not to head directly into space—at least not until they had solved the problem of how to put Superior's inhabitants "ashore" first.

Don, unaccustomed to his new role of interplanetary arbitrator, said tentatively:

"I can't authorize you to take Superior, even if you do put us all ashore, but there must be a comparable piece of Earth we could let you have."

"But Superior is not all," Rezar said. "To use one of your nautical expressions, Superior merely represents a shakedown cruise. Our ability to detach such a populated center has shown the feasibility of raising other typical communities —such as New York, Magnitogorsk and Heidelberg—each a different example of Earth culture."

Don heard a gasp from the Pentagon—or it might have come from the White House.

"You mean you've burrowed under each one of those 'communities'?" Don asked.

Rezar shrugged. "Kaliz's faction," he said, as if to dissociate himself from the project of removing some of Earth's choicest property. "They aim at a history-museum of habitable worlds."

"Interplanetary souvenirs," Alis said. "With quick-frozen inhabitants? Don, what are you going to do?"

Don didn't even know what to say. His eyes met Hector's.

"Don't look at me," Hector said. "I definitely abdicate."

"Look," Don said to Rezar, "how far advanced are these plans? I mean, is there a deadline for this mass levitation?"

"Twenty-four hours, your time," Rezar said.

"Can't you stop them? Aren't you the boss?"

The alien turned Don's question back on him. "Are *you* the boss?"

Don had started to shake his head when Foghorn Frank's voice boomed out.

"Yes, by thunder, he *is* the boss! Don, raise your right hand. I'm going to make you a brigadier general. No, blast it, a full general. Repeat after me . . ."

General Don Cort squared his shoulders. He was almost getting used to these spot promotions.

"Now negotiate," Fogarty said. "You hear me, Mr. Gizl-Rezar? The United States of America stands behind General Cort." There was no audible objection from the White House. "Who stands behind you?"

"A democratic government," Rezar said. "Like yours."

"You represent them?" Fogarty asked.

"With my council, yes."

"Then we can make a deal. Talk to him, Don. I'll shut up now."

Don said to Rezar: "Was it your decision to burrow under New York and Magnitogorsk and Heidelberg?"

"I agreed to it, finally."

"But you agreed to it in the belief that the Earth-people were a warring people and that your old prohibitions did not apply. But we are not a warring people. Earth is at peace."

"Is it?" Rezar asked sadly. "Your plane warred on the submarine."

"In self-defense," Don said. "Don't forget that we defended you, too. And we'd do it again—but not unless provoked."

Rezar looked thoughtful. He tapped his long fingernails on the table. Finally he said: "I believe you. But I must talk to my people first, as you have talked to yours. Let us meet later—" he seemed to be making a mental calculation "—in three hours. Where? Here?"

"How about Cavalier?" Alis suggested. "It would be the first important thing that ever happened there."

FOR THE FIRST TIME since Superior took off, all of the town's elected or self-designated representatives met amicably. They gathered in the common room at Cavalier Institute as they waited for Rezar and his council to arrive for the talks which could decide not only the fate of Superior but of New York and two foreign cities as well.

Apparently the Pentagon expected Don to pretend he had authority to speak for Russia and Germany as well as the United States. But could he speak even for the United States, constitutionally? He was sure that Bobby Thebold, comprising one ninety-sixth of that great deliberative body, the Senate, would let him know if he went too far, crisis or no crisis.

The Senator, re-united with Geneva Jervis, sat holding her hand on a sofa in front of the fireplace, in which logs blazed cheerfully. Thebold looked untypically placid. Jen Jervis, completely sober and with her hair freshly reddened, had greeted Don with a cool nod.

Thebold had been chagrined at learning that Don Cort was not the yokel he had taken him for. But he recovered quickly, saying that if there was any one thing he had learned in his Senate career it was the art of compromise. He would go along with the duly authorized representative of the Pentagon, with which he had always had the most cordial of relations.

"Isn't that so, sweetest of all the pies?" he said to Jen Jervis.

Jen looked uncomfortable. "Please, Bobby," she said. "Not in public." The Senator squeezed her hand.

Professor Garet, whose wife and daughter were serving tea, stood with Ed Clark near the big bay window, through which they looked occasionally to see if the Gizls were coming. Maynard Rubach sat in a leather armchair next to Hector Civek, who had discarded his ermine and wore an old heavy tweed suit. Doc Bendy sat off in a corner by himself. He, too, was untypically quiet.

Don Cort, despite his four phantom stars, was telling himself he must not let these middle-aged men make him feel like a boy. Each of them had had a chance to do something positive and each had failed.

"Gentlemen," Don said, "my latest information from Washington confirms that the Gizls have actually tunneled under the cities they say their militant faction want to take up to the asteroid belt, just as they dug in under Superior before it took off. So they're not bluffing."

"How'd we find out about

Magnitogorsk?" Ed Clark asked. "Iron curtain getting rusty?"

Don told him that the Russians, impressed by the urgency of an unprecedented telephone call from the White House to the Kremlin, had finally admitted that their great industrial city was sitting on top of a honeycomb. The telephone conversation had also touched delicately on the subject of the submarine that had been sunk in mid-Atlantic and there had been tacit agreement that the sub commander had exceeded his authority in firing the missiles and that the sinking would not be referred to again.

Maynard Rubach turned away from the window. "Here they come. Three of them. But they're not coming from the direction of the McFerson place."

"They could have come up from under the grandstand," Don said. "Miss Jervis and I found one of their tunnels there. Remember, Jen?"

Jen Jervis colored slightly, and Don was sorry he'd brought it up. "Yes," she said. "I fainted and Don—Mr. Cort—General Cort—helped me."

"I'm obliged to the general," Senator Thebold said.

PROFESSOR GARET went to the door. The three Gizls followed him into the room. Everyone stood up formally. There was some embarrassed scurrying around because no one had remembered that the Gizls required backless chairs to accommodate their tails.

The Gizls, looking remarkably alike, sat close together. Don tentatively addressed the one in the middle.

"Gentlemen," he said, "first it is my privilege to award to you in the name of the President the Medal of Merit in appreciation of your quick action in saving uncounted lives during the submarine incident. The actual medal will be presented to you when we re-establish physical contact with Earth."

Rezar, who, it turned out, was the one in the middle, accepted with a grave bow. "Our regret is that we were unable to prevent the loss of many valuable objects as well," he said.

"Mr. Rezar," Don said, "I haven't been trained in diplomacy so I'll speak plainly. We don't intend to give up New York. Contrary to general belief, there are about eight million people who *do* want to live there. And I'm sure the inhabitants of Heidelberg and Magnitogorsk feel the same way about their cities."

"Then you yield Superior," Rezar said.

"I didn't say that."

"Yield Superior and we will guarantee safe passage to Earth for all its inhabitants. We only want its physical facilities."

"We'll yield the bubble gum

factory to help your dental problem—for suitable reparations," Don said.

"Payment will be made for anything we take. Give us Superior intact, including the factory and Cavalier Institute, and we will transport to any place you name an area of equal size from the planet Mars."

"Mars?" Don said. "That'd be a very valuable piece of real estate for the researchers."

"Take it," Don heard Frank Fogarty say from the Pentagon.

Professor Garet spoke up. "If Cavalier goes, I go with it. I won't leave it."

"And I won't leave you, Osbert," his wife said. "Will there be air up there among the asteroids?"

"We are air-breathers like you," Rezar said. "When we have assembled our planet there will be plenty. You will be welcome, Professor and Mrs. Garet."

"Hector?" Don said. "You're still mayor of Superior. What do you think?"

"They can have it," Hector said. "I'll take a nice steady civil service job with the federal government, if you can arrange to get one for me."

"Hector," Ed Clark said, "I think that sums up why you've never been a howling success in politics. You don't give a damn for the people. All you care about is yourself."

Hector shrugged. "Well, you needn't be so holy-sounding, Eddie-boy," he said. "Why isn't the *Sentry* out this week? I'll tell you why. Because you've been so busy filing to the Trimble-Grayson papers on Thebold's private radio and you haven't had time for anything else. How much are they paying you?"

Ed Clark, deflated, muttered, "News is news."

"Is that what you were doing in Senator Thebold's Gripe Room on the midway?" Don asked Clark. "Making this deal?"

"Now, General," Thebold said. "Would you deprive the people of their right to know? Throughout my Senate career I have carried the torch against government censorship, which is the path to a totalitarian state."

"I'm sure part of the deal was that Clark's copy didn't make you anything less than a hero," Don said.

"Don't be too righteous, young man," Thebold said. " 'Lest ye be judged,' as they say. Are you not at this moment bargaining away a piece of a sovereign state of the sovereign United States? I don't happen to represent Ohio but if I did I would rise in the upper chamber to demand your court-martial."

"At ease, Senator!" Don ordered. "You're not in the upper chamber now. You're on an artificial satellite which at any moment is apt to take off into outer space."

Doc Bendy spoke for the first time: "Oops-a-daisy! You tell 'im, Donny-boy. Soo-perior—the town everybody looks up to."

Don frowned at him. Bendy had sunk deep into his chair in his corner. He acknowledged Don's look with a broad smile that vanished in a hiccup.

"Y' don't have to say it, Donny. I been drinkin'. Ever since Superior looped the looperior and flung me feet over forehead into the bee-yond. Shatterin' experience to have nothin' but a kangaroo-hop between you and eternity. Yop, ol' Bendy's been on a bender ever since. But you carry on, boy. Y' doin' a great job."

"Thanks," Don said in irony. "I guess that completes the roster of those qualified to speak for Superior. Oh, I'm sorry, Dr. Rubach. Did you have something to say?"

But all the portly president of Cavalier had to say, though he said it at great length, was that if Cavalier were taken as part of a package deal, its trustees would have to receive adequate compensation. Professor Garet tugged at his sleeve and said,"Sit down, Maynard. They've already said they'll pay."

Fogarty's voice rumbled at Don: "Let's try to speed things up, General. Close the deal on Superior, at least, before the press gets there."

"The press?"

"The rest of the papers couldn't let the Trimble-Grayson chain keep their exclusive. Clark's going to have lots of company soon. The boys've hired a vertiplane. First one off the assembly line. You've seen it. Lands anywhere."

"Okay, I'll try to hurry it up." To the Gizls Don said: "All right. You take Superior, minus its people, and bring us a piece of Mars."

"Agreed," Rezar said. It was as easy as that. Nobody objected. Too many of Superior's self-proclaimed saviors had been caught with their motives showing.

"You've got to give up New York, though," Don said. He felt as if he were playing a game of interplanetary Monopoly. "We'll give you a chunk of the great central desert instead, if Australia's willing. (Would that come under the South East Asia Treaty Organization, Mr. Secretary?) Complete with kangaroos and assorted wallabies, if you want them."

"Agreed," said Rezar.

Don sighed quietly to himself. It should be smooth sailing now that the hurdle of New York was past.

But Kaliz, the one Alis had called the Bad Gizl, shook his head violently and spoke for the first time. "No," he said firmly.

"We must have New York. It is by far the greatest of our conquests and I will not yield it."

Rezar said sharply, "We have foresworn conquest."

"I tire of your moralizing," Kaliz said. "We are dealing with beings whose greatest respect is for power. If we temporize now we will lose their respect. They will think our new world weak and itself open to conquest. We have the power—let us use it. I say take New York *and* its people and hold them hostage. The city is ready for lifting."

"No!" Don said. "You can't have New York."

Kaliz seemed to smile. "We already have it. It's merely a question of transporting it." He put a long-fingered hand to his furry chest where, almost hidden in the blue-gray fur, was a flat perforated disk. He said into it: "Show them that New York is ours!"

"Wait!" Rezar said.

"Merely a demonstration," Kaliz told him, "for the moment, at least."

Frank Fogarty's voice, alarmed, said urgently: "Tell him we believe him. New York's reporting an earthquake or something very like it. For God's sake tell him to put it back while we re-orient our thinking."

Kaliz nodded in satisfaction. "The city is as it was. Our people under New York raised it a mere fraction of an inch. It could as easily have been a mile. Do not under-estimate our power."

Rezar was agitated. "We came in peace," he said to his fellow Gizl. "Let us not leave in war. There's power on both sides, capable of untold destruction. Neither must use it. We are a democratic people. Let us vote. I say we must not take New York."

"And I say we must," Kaliz told him, "in self-interest."

They turned to the third of their people, who had been looking from one to the other, his eyes reflecting indecision.

Kaliz barked at him: "Well, Ezial? Vote."

Ezial said: "I abstain."

Deadlock.

Don was sweating. He looked at the others in the room. They were tense but silent, apparently willing to leave it up to Don and his link with the Defense Department.

Frank Fogarty's voice said:

"SAC has been airborne in total strength for half an hour, General. It was a purely precautionary alert at the time."

Don started to interrupt.

"I know they hear me," the Secretary of Defense said. "I intend that they should. We don't want to fight but we will if we must. Son—" the rough voice faltered for a moment "—if necessary we'll destroy Superior to kill this alien and save New York. As a soldier I hope you understand. It's the lives of three thousand people against the lives of eight million."

Only Don and the Gizls had heard. Don looked across the room and into Alis's eyes. She gave him a tentative smile, noting his grave expression.

"Yes, sir," Don said finally.

Rezar spoke. "This is folly." He touched the disk in the fur of his own chest.

"No!" Kaliz cried.

"It is time," Rezar said. "We are beginning to fail in our mission." He spoke reverently into the disk: "My lord, awake."

Kaliz said quickly: "Raise New York! Take it up!"

"They will not obey you now," Rezar said. "I have invoked the counsel of the Master."

CHAPTER XXV

THE MAN was frail and incredibly old. He had sparse white hair and a deeply lined face but his eyes were alert and wise. He wore a cloak-like garment of soft, warm-looking material. His expression was one of kindliness but strength.

The doorbell had rung and Mrs. Garet had answered it. The old man had walked slowly into the room, followed respectfully by two Gizls.

"My lord," said Rezar. He got to his feet and bowed, as did the other Gizls. "I had hoped to let you sleep until your new world had been prepared for you. But the risk was great that if I delayed, your world would never be. Forgive me."

"You did well," the old man said.

Don stood up, too, with a sense of awe that this personage inspired. "How do you do, sir," he said.

"How do you do, General Cort."

"You know my name?"

"I know many things. Too many for such a frail old body. But someone had to preserve the heritage of our people and I was chosen."

"Won't you sit down, sir?"

"I'll stand, thanks. I've rested long enough. Generations, as a matter of fact. Shall I answer some of your obvious questions? I'd better say a few things quickly, before Foghorn Frank hits the panic button."

Don smiled. "Can he hear you or shall I repeat everything?"

"Oh, he hears me. I've got gadgets galore, even though I'm between planets at the moment. I must say it's a pleasure to be among people again." He nodded pleasantly around the room.

Mrs. Garet smiled to him. "Would you like a cup of tea?"

"Later, perhaps, thank you. First I must assure you and everyone of Earth that no one will be harmed by us and that we want nothing for our new world that you are not willing to give."

"That's good to hear," Don said. "I gather you've been in some kind of suspended animation since you left your old world. So I wonder how you're able to speak English."

"Everything was suspended but the subconscious. That kept perking along, absorbing everything the Gizls fed into it. And they've been absorbing your culture for ten years, so I'm pretty fluent. And I certainly know enough to apologize for all the inconvenience my associates have caused you in their zeal to re-establish the human race of Gorel-zed. In the case of Kaliz, of course, it was excessive zeal which will necessitate his rehabilitation."

"Your pardon, Master," Kaliz said humbly.

"Granted. But you'll be rehabilitated anyway."

Don asked: "Did I understand you to say you plan to re-establish your race? Do you mean there are more of you, aside from the kangaroo-people?"

"Oh, yes. Young people. The youngest of all from Gorel-zed. They were put to sleep like me, to be ready to carry on when their new world is built. I won't wake them till then. I hope to live that much longer."

"I'm sure you will, sir."

"Kind of you. But let's get on with the horse trading. Of course we won't take New York, or the two other cities." (There was a collection of sighs of relief from Washington.) "But we would like some of your uninhabited jungle land—the lusher the better, to help us out in the oxygen department. We'd also like some of your air, if you can spare it. We've got a planet to supply now, not just ships."

"How would you get air across space?" Don asked.

"At the moment," the Master said, "I'm afraid we're not prepared to barter our scientific knowledge."

"I didn't mean to pry. It just didn't seem to be something you could do. Do you think we could supply them with some air, Mr. Secretary?"

"I'll have to ask the science boys about that one," Frank Fogarty said. "Meanwhile it's okay with Australia on the desert. But your Gizl friends have to agree to relocate the aborigines from that tract, and they must take every last rabbit or it's no deal."

"Agreed," the Master said with a smile. "But please ask their stockmen to hold their fire. My friends only *look* like kangaroos."

As Don and the Master were making arrangements for Superior to touch down so its people could be transferred to Earth, a blaze of light stabbed down from the sky. Through the window they saw the vertiplane settling slowly to the campus.

"It sure beats a blimp," Senator Thebold said in admiration.

Professor Garet got up to look. "It's the press," he said to his wife. "You might as well invite them in. I hope we have enough tea."

The vertiplane's door opened and the first wave of reporters spilled out.

CHAPTER XXVI

As Superior headed back across the Atlantic, the Earth-people were given a farewell tour. For the first time they had an authorized look at the underground domain of the Gizls, which they reached through the tunnel that led below from under Cavalier's grandstand.

The observation room which Don and Jen Jervis had found was connected by a hidden elevator to a vast main chamber. A control console formed the entire wall of one end of it. Half a dozen Gizls stood at the base of the console. From time to time one of them would launch himself upward with his powerful legs, grab a protruding rung, make an adjustment, then drop lightly back to the floor.

Don and Alis stood for a moment watching Professor Garet, who was tugging at his beard as he became aware of the magnitude of the operation which drove Superior through the skies and was soon to take it across space to the asteroid belt.

"Poor father," Alis whispered to Don. "Magnology in action, after all these years—and he didn't have a thing to do with discovering it."

"Is that why he wants to go with the Master?"

"I imagine so. If he stayed on Earth he'd have nothing. He's too old to start again. It's kind of them to take him—and mother. In a way, I suppose, his going is justification for his years of work. He'll at least be close to the things he might have developed in the right circumstances."

"He certainly won't be lonely," Don said. "Have you noticed the rush to emigrate? Cheeky McFerson's decided to stick with his bubble gum factory. He says the Gizls are a ready-made market. He saw one of them cram five Super-Bubs into his mouth at one time. That's twenty-five cents right there."

Alis giggled. "And half the student body of Cavalier wants to go. You'd think they'd be disillusioned with father. But they're not—I guess they had to be crazy to enroll in the first place."

"Senator Thebold's started campaigning to be named U. S. ambassador to Superior. I heard him talking to the man from *The New York Times*. I suspect they'll give it to him—they'll need his influence to get Senate approval of the treaty with the Gizls."

"I had a little talk with Jen Jervis," Alis said. "She's radiant, have you noticed? The Senator finally asked her to marry him. That's all that was the matter with her—Bobby the Bold had left her hanging by her thumbs too long."

"I guess he did." Don sought a way to get the conversation away from Jen Jervis. "Where's Doc Bendy? He certainly turned out to be a disappointment."

"Poor Doc!" Alis said. "He's always the first to form a committee. But then his enthusiasm wears off and he goes back to the bottle. Only now he's got a keg."

Don snapped his fingers. "The keg. I almost forgot about that matter duplicator. If it can give you perfume and Doc rum—Come on; let's reopen negotiations with the Master."

They found the old man surrounded by a group of reporters, being charmingly evasive with the science editor of *Time*. Professor Garet had now joined this group, where he listened as eagerly as a student.

The Master was showing them the vault-like chamber in which he had spent the generations since the spaceships left Gorelzed. He let them examine the coffin-sized drawer that had been his bed and indicated the others where the younger ones still slept, awaiting the birth of their new planet. Don counted fewer than three dozen drawers.

"Is that all?" he asked.

"Infants and children take up less room," the Master said. "There are two or three in each drawer, and still others in the ships that never came to Earth. Even so, we number fewer than a thousand."

"But you have the matter duplicator," Don said. "Won't it work on people?"

"Unfortunately, no. Transsubstantiation has never worked on living cells. Don't think we haven't tried. We shall have to encourage early marriages and hope for a high birth rate."

"Now about this transsubstantiator," the *Time* man said, and Garet's head cocked in delight, apparently at the resounding sound of the word, "what's the principle? You don't have to give away the secret—just give me a general idea."

The Master firmly shook his head.

Don asked, "What will you trade for the transsubstantiator and the paralysis sceptre you gave Hector?"

The old man smiled. "Not even New York," he said. "Our moral code couldn't permit us to trade either. Earth has enough problems already."

"Offer him the formula for fusion," Frank Fogarty's voice said from the Pentagon.

The old man shuddered. "I heard that," he said. "No, thank you, Mr. Secretary!"

"This is the *clean* bomb," Fogarty said. "It ought to come in very handy in construction work on your new planet."

"We will try to manage in our own way," the Master said. He asked Garet: "Wouldn't you say that Magnology was sufficient for our purposes, Professor?"

Alis' father beamed at being consulted and hearing his own term applied to the Gorel-zed propulsion system.

"More than sufficient," he said enthusiastically. "Preferable, in fact. Magnology is safe, stressless and permanently powerful in stasis. It is the ultimate in gravity-beam nullification. If anything can glue the asteroids back into the planet they once were, Magnology will do it. You can understand how I was misled. Your system so fitted my theory that I imagined it was I who had caused Superior to rise from Earth."

"I understand perfectly," the Master replied graciously. "And I cannot say how glad I am that you and Mrs. Garet have chosen to stay with Cavalier and Superior and become citizens of our new world."

"What will you call your new planet?" the AP man asked. "Asteroida? Something like that?"

"We haven't decided. I welcome suggestions."

The UP man was inspired. "How about Neworld?" he asked. "That describes it perfectly, doesn't it? New world—Neworld?" He wrote it on a piece of paper and admired it.

"Thank you," the Master said. "We'll certainly consider it."

The UP man was satisfied. He had a lead for his story.

SUPERIOR, Nov. 6 (INS)—The floating city of Superior, Earthbound again after nearly six days of aerial meandering, prepared today to discharge its former residents. Its new inhabitants, the kangaroo-like Gizls who came from beyond the stars to swing an unprecedented barter deal involving the United States, Russia and Germany, said they would leave almost immediately to join Superior with the new planet they have been building in the asteroid belt between Mars and Jupiter. . . .

HEIDELBERG, Nov. 6 (AP)—This university city said goodbye today to some 400 interplanetary visitors it belatedly realized had long been burrowed under it. The first officially acknowledged flying saucer landed on Heidelberg's outskirts early today and took aboard the Gizls, who, but for the shrewd maneuvering of the U. S. Secretary of State, "Foghorn

Frank" Fogarty, acting through a hastily-commissioned ex-sergeant troubleshooter, General Don Cort . . .

MOSCOW, Nov 6 (Reuters)—The industrial city of Magnitogorsk was assured of remaining Soviet territory today with the departure of 1,000 kangaroo-like aliens. These visitors from Gorel-zed, the doomed world whose survivors will increase the number of planets in the Solar System to ten with the creation between Mars and Jupiter of . . .

HARTFORD, CONN., (NANA)—Altitude-induced eccentricity has been suggested as a possible explanation for the weird behavior of Superior's inhabitants during its sojourn in the sky. Dr. Harris Byroad, chief surgeon of a leading insurance company, says an ascent from sea level to altitudes of 20,000 feet throws a strain on the nervous system, resulting from a lack of sufficient oxygen to nourish the brain tissues. This causes certain normally stable people to go through periods of flighty judgment and eccentric behaviorism. . . .

From the editorial page of The New York *Daily News:*

NICE KNOWING YOU, GIZLS, BUT—

Next time you visit us, how about doing it openly, instead of burrowing underground like a bunch of Reds? . . .

BULLETIN

ABOARD THE SPACESHIP SUPERIOR, Nov 6 (UP)—This former Ohio town, adapted for space travel, took off for the asteroid belt today after transferring 2,878 of its citizens to a convoy of buses bound for a relocation center. The other 122 of its previous population of 3,000 chose to remain aboard to pioneer the birth of the tenth planet of the Solar System—Neworld.

Neworld, named by the United Press correspondent accompanying the survivors of the burned-out planet of Gorel-zed, will become the second known inhabited planet in the Solar System . . .

CHAPTER XXVII

"JUST A MINUTE, Alis," Don said.

"No, sir, Sergeant-General Donald Cort, sir. Not a minute longer. You tell him now."

"All right. Sir," Don Cort (Gen., temp.) said to Frank Fogarty, Secretary of Defense, "has the mission been accomplished?"

Don and Alis were in the back seat of an army staff car that was leading the bus convoy.

"Looks that way, son. Our best telescopes can't see them any more. I'd say Neworld was well on its way to a-borning."

Alis Garet, her arms around Don and her head on his shoulder, spoke directly into the transceiver. "Mr. Fogarty, are you aware that I haven't had a single minute alone with this human radio station since I've known him? This is the most inhibited man in the entire U. S. Army."

"Miss Garet," the Defense Secretary said, "I understand perfectly. When I was courting Mrs. Fogarty I was a pilot on the Meseck Line— Well, never mind that. Mission accomplished, General Cort, my boy."

"Then, sir," Don said, "Sergeant Cort respectfully requests permission to disconnect this blasted invasion of privacy so he can ask Miss Alis Garet if she thinks two of us can live on a noncom's pay."

The driver of the staff car, a sergeant himself, said over his shoulder: "Can't be done, General."

Fogarty said: "Don't be too anxious to revert to the ranks, my boy. I'll admit the T/O for generals isn't wide open but I'm sure we can compromise somewhere between three stripes and four stars. Suppose you take a ten-day delay en route to Washington while we see what we can do. I'll meet you in the White House on November 16. The President tells me he wants to pin a medal on you."

"Yes, sir," Don said. Alis was very close and he was only half listening. "Any further orders, sir?"

"Just one, Don. Kiss her for me, too. Over to you."

"Yes, sir!" Don said. "Over and out."

∞ ∞ ∞

BACK ISSUES

Royal Publications, Inc., is now in a position to supply back issues of *Infinity* and Science *Fiction Adventures*. All issues are available with the single exception (at the moment) of Volume 1, Number 1, of *Infinity*. In case you've missed any issues, here's a checklist. It's impossible to list the complete contents of each issue, but we do want to remind you of some of the "must" items each one has contained:

INFINITY SCIENCE FICTION

February, 1956; Vol. 1, No. 2	*The Best of Fences* by Randall Garrett
June, 1956; Vol. 1, No. 3	*The Guests of Chance* by Beaumont & Oliver
August, 1956; Vol. 1 No. 4	*The Big Fix* by Richard Wilson; *Someday* by Isaac Asimov
October, 1956; Vol. 1, No. 5	*The Silver Corridor* by Harlan Ellison
December, 1956; Vol. 1 No. 6	*The Superstition-Seeders* by Edward Wellen
February, 1957; Vol. 2, No. 1	*Hunt the Hog of Joe* by Robert Ernest Gilbert
April, 1957; Vol. 2, No. 2	*Friends and Enemies* by Fritz Leiber
June, 1957; Vol. 2, No. 3	Novelets by Lester del Rey and Robert F. Young
July, 1957; Vol. 2, No. 4	*The Men Return* by Jack Vance
September, 1957; Vol. 2, No. 5	*Dio* by Damon Knight; three satellite stories by Arthur C. Clarke
October, 1957; Vol. 2, No. 6	Clarke, Garrett, McLaughlin, Kornbluth, Simak, and others
November, 1957; Vol. 3, No. 1	*The General and the Axe* by Gordon R. Dickson
January, 1958; Vol. 3, No. 2	*And Then the Town Took Off* (Part I) by Richard Wilson; *Lenny* by Isaac Asimov

SCIENCE FICTION ADVENTURES

December, 1956; Vol. 1, No. 1	*The Starcombers* by Edmond Hamilton
February, 1957; Vol. 1, No. 2	*Slaves of the Star Giants* by Robert Silverberg
April, 1957; Vol. 1 No. 3	*Clansmen of Fear* by Henry Hasse
June, 1957; Vol. 1, No. 4	*Chalice of Death* by Calvin M. Knox
August, 1957; Vol. 1, No. 5	*This World Must Die!* by Ivar Jorgenson
September, 1957; Vol. 1, No. 6	*The Slave* by C. M. Kornbluth
October, 1957; Vol. 2, No. 1	*Thunder Over Starhaven* (book-length novel) by Ivar Jorgenson
December, 1957; Vol. 2, No. 2	*Valley Beyond Time* by Robert Silverberg
January, 1958; Vol. 2, No. 3	*Hunt the Space-Witch!* by Ivar Jorgenson

The price is 35¢ each, any 3 for $1.00. If your order totals $1.00 or more, we will pay the postage; otherwise, please include 5¢ per magazine to cover handling and mailing. Send your check or money order to Royal Publications, Inc., 11 West 42nd Street, New York 36, New York.

By the editor

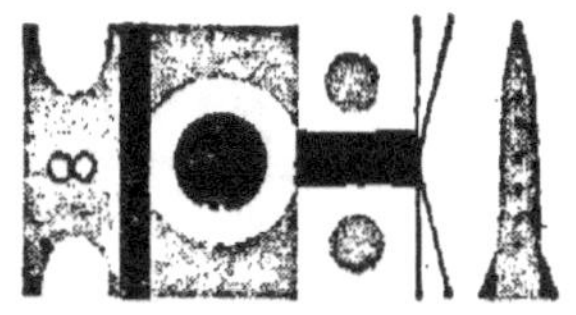

ANY OLD BRAINS FOR SALE?

THERE is a tradition in several kinds of fiction that might be called the "bully" legend. You can find it, among other places, in books for boys, light love stories, and science fiction. You know how it goes: the tough kid down the block, or the handsome athlete, or the evil dictator pushes everybody around until the physically weaker but much more clever hero shows him up for the stupid clod that he is.

It's an attractive vision—particularly attractive to people who are "bookish" to begin with and do more reading than the bully types they hate and/or envy. But it doesn't work out very well in real life, and if recent psychological findings didn't demolish it, the launching of Sputnik certainly should.

Unfortunately, the bully turns out to have brains, too. Brains just as good as the hero's, and apparently better oiled. The bully not only has a helluva fine pitching arm; he knows how—and when—to use it!

And the hero who was sitting back smugly saying, "We'll lick 'em when the time comes!" suddenly finds that the time has come and gone, and he is running like mad to catch up.

Part of the trouble, I think, is that we have always been willing to praise "cleverness" but never quite prepared to trust *brains*. The stereotype of the ivory-tower scientist is well-known, and as false to fact as those of the stupid bully and the clever hero. But it's natural that there should be a stereotype of some sort, because apparently most people have only the vaguest kinds of ideas about what scientists are and do.

In 1947, the National Opinion Research Center asked a nation-wide cross-section of people a number of questions in order to find out something about basic public attitudes towards various occupations. One of the occupations included was nuclear physicist, and 51% of the people interviewed admitted they didn't know enough about the job to rate its value. To find out what they *did* know about it, NORC asked a second, carefully phrased question: "A good many people don't know exactly what a nuclear physicist does, but what is your general idea of what he does?"

In this case, only 3% gave a satisfactorily exact definition or explanation. Eighteen percent gave partially correct answers, 17% were vague ("physicist," "scientist," and the like), 7% were wrong, and 55% "didn't know." Some of the wrong answers are worth quoting.* For instance:

"Assistant to a physic. His job would be on the body."

"He does something at an operation—I think he gives the anaesthetic."

"I think 'nuclear' is some kind of new plastic."

"He determines the relation of different matters to other matters."

"He's a spy."

"Studies eggs, doesn't he?"

"He's a corsetier."

"He's a man who washes windows."

"It's one of those people who reads minds and tells things by the stars."

"He replaces your limbs when they've been amputated."

"A persuader."

"Maybe it's what you're doing—finding out what people think."

"Studies bugs, I think."

"Something to do with the New Dealers."

"He's a doctor that puts you to sleep and makes you talk about yourself."

It should be emphasized that this survey was taken ten years ago. Nuclear physicists were newer then than they are now, and perhaps a survey taken in 1957 would have had different results. Certainly, more people today should know what a nuclear physicist is and does—if only because so many educators and politicians have been complaining in public that we don't have enough of them.

Nevertheless, the answers quoted are dismaying, even while they're laughable. Sure, *you* know what a nuclear physicist does. (Did somebody say, "He saves the Earth from alien invaders"?) But don't sneer at people who don't. There are reasons why they don't: flaws in our educational system, flaws in our national philosophy, flaws somewhere. Wherever they are, it's about time we got rid of them.

Let's begin by getting rid of stereotypes, wherever we may find them. They're prevalent, as I said, in science fiction; let's ditch them. If we succeed, sf may set a good example for other fiction, and for people generally.

I'm going to try. Will you help?—LTS

*I read these results in a book called **Class, Status and Power; A Reader in Social Stratification**, edited by Reinhard Bendix and Seymour Martin Lipset, published by The Free Press, Glencoe, Illinois.

Feedback

ANYBODY who rereads my Matheson review, and compares it with Mr. Edwards' letter, will see for himself which of the two is "a neurotic, personal attack."

Incidentally, Mr. Edwards writes from 11550½ Friar Street, North Hollywood, California, which happens to be Charles Beaumont's address. Beaumont, if that isn't you, I think you ought to speak up, in order to avoid being confused with this noisy creep.—Damon Knight.

∞

Reference your editorial, November (??) issue . . . "Of course, it would be nice if everybody emulated Mr. Gold instead of Mr. Edwards, at least as far as brevity is concerned" . . . "I like fantasy fine, personally, but the sales figures on every magazine publishing it during the past twenty years give ample proof that most readers don't." End of extended quote.

This merely proves that most readers and editors are slobs. Q.E.D. This also proves that the majority is always wrong. Q.E.D. This solves most of the present problems of human association.

Short enough?—R. C. Crawley, Box 190, Jasper, Alberta, Canada.

Too short. Meaning?—LTS.

∞

Ordinarily I avoid picking out insigificant scientific flaws in sf stories, mostly because I feel so vulnerable myself. However, I can't resist picking on James Blish. For one thing, he has one of the best scientific educations in sf so that a flaw in one of his yarns is worth ten elsewhere. For another, in his book reviews he is generally quite merciless toward the scientific shortcomings of others, so he's fair game, isn't he?

In his story "Nor Iron Bars," in the November 1957 issue, Jim says, and I quote: "Outside, the weak 'light' of googols of atomic nuclei vanished, to be replaced instantly with sable and stars."

Well, that means that at least two googols of atomic nuclei were in the vicinity. Two googols, using Kasner and Newman's famous definition of the term, is 2×10^{100}. The lightest atomic nuclei that can exist are individual protons. Now, then, how much is the mass of 2×10^{100} protons? A single proton has a mass, roughly, of 1.7×10^{-24} grams. Two googols of protons, therefore, weigh 3.4×10^{76} grams.

How does this mass compare with that of the universe? Our sun has a mass of about 2×10^{33} grams. Assuming that our sun is an average star and that there are a hundred billion stars in our galaxy; and that our galaxy is an average galaxy and that there are a hundred billion galaxies in the universe; and allowing for a mass of interstellar matter equal to that of all the stars, the total mass of the universe is about 4×10^{55} grams.

That means that two googols of atomic nuclei would represent a mass of matter equal to a billion trillion universes. (1,000,000,000,-000,000,000,000 universes if you want it in figures.)

Surely Jim didn't really mean there were googols of atomic nuclei hanging around.—Isaac Asimov.

∞

I'll come right to the point, as far as I'm concerned knight is still the best damned reviewer and critic in the entire field despite whatever stupid accusation that muck-rakers like F. E. Edwards can think up.

By the way your magazine stinks! — Ronald Musser, 704 North James Street, Carbondale, Illinois.

∞

I've got a few bones to pick. Why can't you make up your mind as to your cover format? I vastly prefer that on the October ish to that on the November ish. For one thing, it is much neater and has better artwork.

On the other hand that red background for November is torture after looking at it for a while, and that typeface—the whole thing has a hurried look. Was that a genuine experiment or a less time-consuming job to meet a deadline? *(Less time would have been consumed by sticking to the October format, but we liked that for November better. How do you like the present one?—LTS)*

The stories, I am happy to say, did not bear out its impression. All were good, the best ones by Blish, Lang and Dickson. Dickson, I think, muffed slightly when he made the assumption, "As New Earth goes, so goes Humanity." Gregor's story was good and had a punchline that is slightly familiar —false memories, reversion to self, etc. Has he been writing any in the last few years? *(Very little, aside from scientific articles.—LTS)* The only other story of his I remember reading was "Heavy Planet" in *Adventures in Time and Space.* Lang's tale was one of those understated things that grows on you. But I still say go back to your October exterior format.—Bill Murphy, 207 South Andre, Saginaw, Michigan.

∞

Here I go again from a third address. I'll try to be short and to the point.

For 113 pages, 623 points on my system. Story average of 5.9, or a hair above C plus on an A to D scale. One of the poorest you've had ever.

B: "The General and the Axe" by Dickson. Only because the ending was halfway decent.

B: "The Long Question" by Mason. Very nice.

B-: "Formula for Murder" by Gregor. Why did you dig up this

antiquarian author? Perhaps he can get up to date. This story was quite juvenile, and only good by comparison with those below.

C: "The Skirmisher" by Budrys.

C: "The Railhead at Kysyl Khoto." This should *never* have been published, as Raymond Jones did it magnificently three times.

C: "Nor Iron Bars" by Blish.

C: "One-Way Journey" by Silverberg.

I agree with Gold, only more so. Who founded the *Galaxy* heavy-handed type of satire (which I don't happen to like)? Some author who wrote "To Serve Man," "Don't Live in the Past," "Cabin Boy," "Special Delivery," "World Without Children," etc., etc., etc. (Some of his I like, too.) Who? Damon Knight, in person and pen.

Criticism of the critic Department: The review of Vance's book was fair, the type that *all* must be in a magazine of your type. That of *The Green Odyssey* was very, very bad. I consider this novel the utmost blend of space opera, pure science fiction, adventure fiction, entertainment and anthropological fiction. That "(honest)" was silly, as the mowers made fine sense on a space port planet for a tremendous civilization which came before Man. And how could spaceships land on *water* in an "ocean"? Just because Farmer doesn't let Questions of all sorts get in the way of the story is no reason for condemning the book. Dick got somewhat better treatment, but not a review, but only criticism which has no place in INFINITY.

The cover was very poor, though I see that Emsh didn't have anything in the text to illustrate well. How about a symbolic cover like on the latest ASF?—Roland Hirsch, Noah Hall Room 319, Oberlin College, Oberlin, Ohio.

∞

1. This is to certify that the following officers have been elected in the World Science Fiction Society, Inc. to serve from November 1, 1957 to October 31, 1958:

Anna Sinclare Moffatt, President
Len J. Moffatt, Secretary
Rick Sneary, Treasurer
Stan Woolston, Printing and Publicity
Forrest J Ackerman, Professional Public Relations
George W. Fields, Fan Public Relations.

2. This is to certify that the following two Directors were elected to serve from November 1, 1957 to October 31, 1960:

Belle C. Dietz
David Neuman.

3. This is to certify that the 16th Annual World Science Fiction Convention will be held over the Labor Day weekend, 1958, at the Alexandria Hotel, Los Angeles, California.

4. Those who wish to join the World Science Fiction Society, Inc. for the current year should send their $1.00 dues to Len J. Moffatt, 10202 Belcher, Downey, California.—Franklin M. Dietz Jr., Recorder-Historian, World Science Fiction Society, Inc., 1721 Grand Avenue, Bronx 53, New York.

∞

INFINITY, Vol. 3, No. 1. Your

third year is starting off fairly well. Of the short stories, Blish's sequel to "Detour" and Lang's "Railhead at Kysyl Khoto" were the strongest. The Blish short was unusually good for a follow-up story, even though he pulled a fat rabbit out of the hat to get to the point. Lang's thing has a most interesting currency in that it was written and published before friend—rather, Comrade Sputnik showed up. What ever happens now, it will always be remembered that we were *second*, where the Russians were up there firstest with the mostest (in this case, lead).

Of the novelets, Dickson's "General and the Axe" was definitely the best in the issue. It read like another ASF-type, where hero is in the spot of having to make a decision for the general good that serves only to gain the utter hate of the whole fan damily. However, this time Dickson carried the fate of the general to its logical conclusion, rather than soften the thing at the end. I liked the story. Neither Silverberg's nor Gregor's stories were particularly interesting, in my opinion. Gregor had a message, but I don't think he got it off except in the last two sentences.

After I just got through praising you to the skies for your new cover logo, you went back to a left-of-center style. I must say, in all fairness, that the *new* new look is best of all. I like the kaleidoscope on SFA better, but that stuff would be out of place except on an adventure magazine.—J. Martin Graetz, 32 Fayette Street, Cambridge 39, Massachusetts.

∞

Way back in your third issues (of INFINITY) you said: "If there's any writer you think should be included in the list, no matter how seldom he has appeared or how long ago he was heard from, let me know, and I'll do my best to make him produce."

Hold on to your hat.

You've got Edward E. Smith, Ph. D. Fine! Only tell him to throw Kinnison out the window. We wanna hear about the galaxy's only Vortex Blaster, "Storm" Cloud. Ed Earl Repp, for his interplanetaries. John Russell Fearn, for something like "Liners of Time." Stanton A. Coblentz, for his magnificent satires. Robert Moore Williams, for anything. Ross Rocklynne, something like the "Darkness" series. Polton Cross, for his "Man from Hell," which was a masterpiece, and I dare anyone to defy me. Eando Binder. Oh! For another "After an Age." Manly Wade Wellman, Frederick Kummer, Isaac Asimov. . . . Well, that's enough for now.

I know I'm asking an awful lot, Ed, but even half of these authors would give you leadership in the action-packed stf field.—Don Kent, 3800 Wellington, Chicago, Illinois.

To be honest, I'll be lucky if I do get stories out of half of these authors. But you seem to have been brought up on the same kind of sf I was, and you've given me a good idea of the kind of story you like. Rest assured that I'll do my best to keep you satisfied. And don't hesitate to let me know if you have any other requests.—LTS.

∞

You folks have a new Art Director, and it may yet appear, a good one. He is not batting 1000 yet, though, so please transmit this reader's eye view for his better information.

On the good side, Kluga is a real artist and uses the available medium intelligently—has good line, design, page variety, mood, imagination—can be subtle without in any way doubtful and thus is an asset to the text and the effect of the whole, without being too difficult for the lipreaders or too irksomely cliche for the perceptive. This is certainly a lot, and one could say more—but why try to teach a man his business when he so obviously knows it—as an illustrator.

But the question is: does he know or can he learn all the other duties which fall to the lot of a magazine Art Director?

Most of your other illustrators continue to get away with murder to the text, and Kluga is himself not entirely blameless except when he is carefully vague, allowing the reader to fill in details to please himself and/or the author. Such illustrations at least don't try to enforce inaccuracy on the pained attention of the reader.

Considering what wonderful stories you have been finding and running, illustrative sins are a bad blot which shows up the worse for appearing on so shiny a scutcheon.

Now, for instance, look at the illo, signed Kluga, to Lee Gregor's story. Formula for murder, indeed. I will bet up to 3¢, cash or stamp, that he had that thing kicking around for half a year or more before he ever saw the story. Oh! where was your blue pencil? Had he openly confessed to you, or had you been at all alert, you might have blue-pencilled the heroine from the author's "squarish blonde" to a curvaceous brunette and all had been well. But no; you were trustingly asleep and Kluga had not quite nerve enough to tell you the original subtitle, which as near as I can read at this telepathic distance in space-time, erasure and dismay, was: "Harlan traduces me, Larry," she sobbed tempestuously, "I am always courteous even to baldheaded artists."

But from blonde to brunette is not the worst, drastic though at first glance it does seem. Maybe the style changed within the week or less the story's action took—women do change their minds and heads. At least, the brunette is nice looking in her own right. But what about Bowman's work on Silverberg's text? Where, oh, where was your blue pencil *then*? Change the shape of the head from broad to pointed; the nose from a grotesque bubble to a grotesque drip; face from wide to narrow; skin from brown to white; shoulders from broad to narrow; mouth from a circle to a horseshoe and cut the number of openings in half. Since the author says that the potatosack gown goes all the way down to the thick ankles, you might have put in a footnote to the effect that the ankles are so thick that they go all the way up to the knee, thus hauling your text into some alignment with the illo.

Though I vaguely suspect that readers buy mags to read stories and therefore wonder where the artists head in to be grabbing off the sayso in this highhanded manner.

I could go on and on—Emsh reducing the General's spaceships from five to four—the railhead at Kysyl Khoto with no backstop, the trains would shoot off onto the sand; has this Schoenherr never seen a railroad siding on the outworld he was raised on? *(Well now, you know how primitive those Russians are!—LTS)*

But I can no longer look and refrain from weeping. Enough. Too much.

Beat up Kluga and then give him a club and tell him to pass it on where it will do the most good.—Alma "The Heller" Hill, 14 Pleasant Street, Fort Kent, Maine.

∞

I know a real good story.

"The General's Axe" was undoubtedly, and with a whipsting, the best story that I've yet read in INFINITY. I admired the author's slick way of handling the details, not to mention the failures, setbacks and etc. I still remember Harlan Ellison's "Deeper Than Darkness" and can say that it stands with one of the best. Also, there has been a lot of good stories, too, crammed into one of the best magazines on the market today.

Hats off again to "Feedback," the best letter section, ever.—James W. Ayers, 609 First Street, Attalla, Alabama.

∞ ∞ ∞

CAPTAIN FUTURE
WIZARD OF SCIENCE
COMET
FICTION AND FACT OF THE PRIZE-RING
FIGHT STORIES
THE BLACK UHLAN
HEADQUARTERS DETECTIVE
MURDER TREADMILL
G-MAN JUGGERNAUT
MASKED RIDER WESTERN
BORROWED HOSSES
FIGHTING ACES OF WAR SKIES
WINGS
10 STORY WESTERN MAGAZINE
ADVENTURE NOVELS
Thrilling Stories of the Sky Trails
Air STORIES
THE NIGHT HAWK
GEORGE BRUCE
FIGHTING DAREDEVILS OF TODAY'S WAR
AIR WAR
THE ALL-STORY
WARLORD of MARS
ARMY Romances
BASKETBALL STORIES
Battle Stories
O'LEARY IN ACTION IN ETHIOPIA
BLACK BOOK DETECTIVE
GOLDEN FLEECE
HIGH-SEAS ADVENTURES
THE SEA ROGUE
INDIAN Stories
BRIDE of the TOMAHAWK PACK
MY LIFE WITH SITTING BULL
LONE RANGER
MAGIC CARPET MAGAZINE
PEARLS FROM MACAO
MARVEL SCIENCE STORIES
NEW DETECTIVE
North-West ROMANCES
GIRLS of WHITE WATER TRAIL
Oriental Stories
PHANTOM DETECTIVE
PLANET stories
QUEEN OF THE MARTIAN CATACOMBS
POPULAR DETECTIVE
DEATH IN A COTTAGE
PRIVATE DETECTIVE
LOVE STORIES OF THE REAL WEST
RANCH ROMANCES
Maid of the Valley
RANGE RIDERS
SIX-GUN VALLEY
Vice Squad DETECTIVE
SECRET of the HOUSE of HORROR
TOP-NOTCH STORIES ... TOP-NOTCH WRITERS
UNDERWORLD DETECTIVE
FIVE FATAL MINUTES
KILLER BAIT
THRILLING WONDER STORIES
THE FEDERALS IN ACTION
G-MEN
GIVE 'EM HELL
SCIENCE FICTION
SPICY-ADVENTURE STORIES
HELL'S RIVER

—continued from Back Cover

www.ingramcontent.com/pod-product-compliance
Lightning Source LLC
LaVergne TN
LVHW091005080826
845145LV00003B/1130

* 9 7 8 1 6 4 7 2 0 3 7 9 5 *